ORDINARY LIVES

A Collection of Short Stories and A Novella
By Mark Munger

Publishing Writers from the Lake Superior Basin
Duluth, Minnesota

ISBN 0-9720050-0-5
Library of Congress Number applied for

Published by Cloquet River Press:
5353 Knudsen Road
Duluth, Minnesota 55803
(218) 721-3213

Visit the publisher at: www.cloquetriverpress.com
Email the author at: Mlitlgator@msn.com

Printed by InstantPublisher.com
Cover Art and Design by Rene' Munger

For My Aunt and Mentor,
Susanne Schuler

ACKNOWLEDGMENTS

I'm indebted to three individuals who shared time away from their busy lives and schedules to proofread the manuscript for this collection.

Many thanks to Ken Hubert, a life-long friend and dedicated public school teacher for his input. I extend my heartfelt appreciation to Rachel Fulkerson of the *Friends of the Minneapolis Library* for her literary expertise and assistance. Additionally, I'd like to acknowledge the thoughtful reflections of Rev. Stephen Schaitberger, Canon Missioner to Northern Minnesota for the Episcopal Diocese of Minnesota. Without the careful review of this book by these volunteers, many errors and mistakes would have gone undetected.

Finally, I sincerely appreciate the kind words and encouragement received from Charlie Wilkins and Sarah Stonich, two great writers nice enough to listen to me during those times when things weren't going so well.

Mark Munger
Duluth, Minnesota
March 27, 2002

TABLE OF CONTENTS

Duplicity: A Novella   6

Short Stories
Fresh Air   57
Tragedy at Vermillion Falls   64
Waiting for Emily   70
The Beginning Room   78
On the Road   82
Funeral for a Fat Woman   99
The Enlightenment of Howard Bell   104
Ida's Last Christmas   112
Faith   116
Reunion   124
The Ice Cream Parlor   134
Quantico   139
Islands   143
Redemption   168
Easter in the Sangre De Cristos   170
Cuyuna Angel   175
A Quiet Man   188
Sterling, Colorado   196

DUPLICITY: A Novella

CHAPTER 1

The chat room was alive with tension. I stared at the narrative scrolling down the screen of my laptop. Strangers said things to strangers that they would never dream of saying on the street or in a bar unless half drunk. And even then, it would be unlikely that the participants would express themselves so freely. The relative anonymity of the Internet, the ability to create a fictional self in one's Internet Profile and do it all within the impersonal, safe context of typing words upon a screen; words which could then be spun out into the world seemingly without consequence, created an atmosphere of freedom.

"how's it going?"

"great. read your profile. what kind of things do you write?"

I was engaged in a chat with a woman (I presumed she was a woman since nothing on the Internet is real or verifiable) from Canada in a "Writer's Chat" room. I hadn't read her profile to see who or what she claimed to be. I only knew her tone of voice, if the written word across a computer screen conveyed by telephone cable can be said to carry "a tone of voice", was intriguing.

Though the title of the room, "Writer's Chat Forum", gave the impression that the serious business of creative writing was the impetus for the room's existence, the actual content of the discussion was universally more personal, more sensual, than the location's moniker suggested.

"i've written a few short stories. nothing published as yet. i've also tried a novel. no luck there either."

"what's the novel about?"

"it's a murder mystery set in the black hills, where I'm from."

My profile revealed that I lived "in the Midwest". I realized that I'd just inadvertently narrowed my location down considerably.

Other dialogue cluttered the screen, bypassing our conversation. I was new to the chat game. I'd only been online for a few months and didn't know the ins and outs, the etiquette, the tricks of the trade so to speak. Sting29's name became lost in the blur of conversation between other participants in the room. The clock struck. It was near midnight. My wife Beth, newly the mother of our second daughter, was sound asleep in our bed. I recognized that I should be by her side, comforting her after a long day of failed breast-feeding and attempts to subdue a colicky child. Guilt slid across me like a storm cloud but carried with it an edge of unanticipated excitement.

"tax35, are you still there?"

She broke through the idle chatter of the other participants and found me.

"yep. :)." (The "smiley face" was one of the only chat tricks that I knew).

"i thought you deserted me. :(," she responded.

"nope. just got lost in the shuffle."

"did you mean scuffle? lol."

The woman, if that's what she was, had a sense of humor. Captivated, I pulled up her profile:

Name: Roxanne

Age: Somewhere between 20 and 40

Occupation: Professional something or other

Married: Yes, but that doesn't stop me from flirting.

Computer: Some old thing the cat dragged in.

Interests: Poetry, writing, love and religion (I'm Jewish but always interested in other forms of monotheism) and being a mom to my kid.

Quote: "Roxanne, you don't have to put on the red light..." (If you don't know the song, don't bother.)

"great profile."

"what did you like about it?"

"seems fresh and honest."

":). that's me."

Bing.

I knew that the ring of chimes meant something. I just didn't know what.

"i just heard something like chimes."

"YOU DOLT! that was me trying to talk to you privately by instant message."

"you don't have to shout! i'm new at this stuff-you need to go easy on me. tell me how i access it."

"there should be an icon at the top of your screen for im. click on it and you'll see what I wrote."

It took a few moments to figure out how to get to her missive.

"i'm waiting," she wrote across the chat room screen.

I pulled up her instant message.

"hi. i'm rox? what's your real name?"

My profile simply said I was male, thirty-five and married, along with some boring stuff about me being a would-be, wanna-be writer.

I hesitated. Who was this person? Should I remain my normal, cautious self when dealing with women other than my spouse? Maybe this person translating her thoughts into computer blips was a crazed man or woman out to do my family harm. Or someone just out to mess with my mind.

Bing.

"i'm waiting."

My heart was palpitating in ways that it hadn't since I began dating Beth. The excitement of the chase, of the moment, captured reason and beat my psyche into compliance.

I found the function key and turned the chimes off. I sent an Instant Message back to Roxanne with-no-last name:

"my name's michael. my friends call me mike."

"pleased to meet you mike. what do you do when you're not writing stories?"

9

Another question that alarmed my sense of privacy. As if she read my mind, she interjected and revealed something about herself, something not in her profile:

"i'm a lawyer in ontario, canada."

A lawyer. *Female lawyers, aren't by and large, crazy,* I reasoned. *She must be legit,* I thought. *I'll give her the benefit of the doubt.*

"i'm an accountant. pretty boring stuff."

"what kind of accountant?"

"a damn good one!:)"

"lol. i had that coming. i mean, what kind of clients?"

Hmmm. Getting a little personal there, I thought.

Oh what the hell. In the quiet of my living room, I sat considering a response. The grandfather clock in the foyer chimed. It was 12:30 am. I had to work at 7:00.

"i audit hospitals and medical clinics."

"so we have something in common. i represent hospitals that get sued. you make sure i don't give away their money."

"lol. yep. i'm the bastard that checks to make sure all the i's are dotted and all the t's are crossed."

There was a pause in our discussion. I had maximized the Instant Message screen, obliterating all of the other conversations in the chat room. I rubbed my eyes. The length of the day was beginning to overcome the excitement of the encounter.

"what kind of music do you like?"

"mostly rock, though i also like blues," I responded.

"what about sting?"

"he's all right. i like 'every breath you take'. that's a classic. and of course, i'm partial to 'roxanne'."

It was a bold move, a calculated play, made perhaps too early in the game. But I was near the end of my endurance. Even the adrenaline of the moment could not sustain me much longer.

"that's sweet.:)"

"how about you?"

"same, though more into folk. some of that blues stuff gets too pretentious."

She was working her way deeper into my mind. I tried to imagine what she looked like. Was she tall, thin, and metropolitan like I imagined? Darkly Jewish and uninhibited? Dangerous in a certain way, a forbidden woman for a Gentile man? Did she smoke? What did she like to drink?

She was married. Why was she up, late at night, later still because of the time difference, talking to someone in another country when she should be asleep next to the man she loved, just like I should be asleep next to the mother of my children?

Elizabeth was up. I listened quietly, subdued by nervous shame, as the bathroom door closed behind her.

"i need to go to bed."

"me too. too bad you're so far away."

Wow. A direct pitch I hadn't seen coming.

"i meant i have to get up early tomorrow. i'm tired, need to sleep."

"oh. i must be boring you."

I couldn't tell if she was teasing or seriously hurt.

"that's not it. i really do have to get up for work in less than six hours. you're great," I wrote.

"great...that's an interesting choice of words for someone who calls himself a writer."

"pretty lame, i agree. how about intoxicating, intriguing and sensual?"

I knew I was putting myself on the line, opening my privacy up to more than I could likely deal with. I felt the urgency of connection, the ancient rush of sexuality driving my fingers across the keyboard.

"those i'll accept.<puts her arms around the stranger and gives him a deep, romantic first kiss>. sigh."

"can we talk again sometime?"

"sure. i'm free next Tuesday, after 10:00pm your time. how about you?"

I thought for a moment about canceling, about removing myself from the seemingly sorry fantasy I was about to engage in but the mystery of the woman on the other end of the telephone line was irrepressible. It wasn't like I was without a choice. I couldn't claim that. And it wasn't like I was unable to weigh the consequences. I simply couldn't resist.

"ok. i'll look for you around 11:00pm your time in this chat area. i'll bring the wine."

"hmmm. wine. make sure it's red and expensive. i've got just the dress for red wine."

"what's it look like?"

"you'll have to wait. trust me. it'll be worth it. just make sure the wine has a cork."

"you mean no boone's farm or ripple?"

"not if you want to impress this sophisticated lady from thunder bay."

"so noted. i'll make sure the bottle comes with a cork. what should i wear?"

"surprise me. just don't come dressed as an accountant."

"that hurt. don't you like the conservative type?"

"no and i can tell from our conversation that isn't the real you."

"you're pretty sure of yourself, ms. roxanne."

I was entranced. I knew I could sit by the dim light of my computer screen all night and type away fictitious conversation with my non-existent mistress. The toilet flushed. I heard my wife's weary steps retreat across the hardwood towards our bedroom.

"Mike? Are you still up? It's nearly 1:00," Elizabeth called out in a soft voice.

"I'm coming right up."

"gotta go. next tuesday it is. <he returns the kiss with intensity and begins walking towards the shadows.>"

"goodbye, michael <she says, watching him leave through a light rain, asking herself what she's getting into.>"

The bedroom was cold as I undressed. I removed my loose fitting Levi 501's and my T-shirt, trying to be quiet in the exercise, hoping that my wife had gone back to sleep. Slipping on a pair of cotton gym shorts, I found my place under the quilt and sheets on my side of the bed. The chill of winter touched my naked chest as the cold fabric of the bed linens passed over my skin.

"What were you doing up so late?"

There was a hint of suspicion, of mistrust in Beth's voice as her words found my exhausted ears.

"Just researching some material for a story," I replied.

"After midnight?"

"Uh huh. Got carried away. I'll be fine."

But as I tried to sort out what had taken place over the past hour, I began to realize that my last statement was a lie.

CHAPTER 2

I waited until 11:00 PM the following Tuesday. I used the search features on my browser in an attempt to locate Roxanne. The screen of my notebook told me she was not online, that she had missed our date. Disappointed, I shut the machine down.

I had actually bought a bottle of red wine, a nice Beringer from the Napa Valley, complete with cork, for the occasion. I was dressed in my best black Lee jeans and a neatly pressed muted green dress shirt.

A fire circled anxiously around a birch log behind the clear glass doors of our fireplace. Picking up my wineglass by its cool stem, I walked contemplatively to an over-stuffed sofa and sat heavily before the flames. Beth was upstairs making sure Anna, our oldest, was in bed. Jessie, the baby, murmured contentedly in her crib. The wine tasted of sweet grapes and warmed the recesses of my mouth with its afterglow.

I pondered why I was so intrigued by words written by someone I'd never met. I asked myself how a sensible, mature father of two could become so infatuated with an idea, for that was really all Roxanne was; a mere concept, a capricious specter of femininity. The more I thought about the awkwardness of my feelings, the worse my self-loathing became. The wine didn't seem to help. I vowed to keep the damned computer turned off, to avoid its evil hold on my soul, as I drained the last of the liquor and climbed the stairs to sleep.

"why weren't you online last night?"

"i'm sorry. something came up."

"what?"

"it's personal."

"how so?"

There was a pause in our conversation. Despite my best attempts to remain Internet free, my self-prohibition lasted less than 24 hours. An intense desire to connect, to feel like a teenager again, to flee responsibilities, obligations, and the mundane, drove me to the computer screen on Wednesday while Elizabeth and the girls were out shopping.

"my husband doesn't appreciate the amount of time I spend in chat rooms."

"rooms?"

"there are more places to talk than this one, you know."

"and i thought i was special.:(."

"you are. but you can't get on a girl for checking out alternatives, can you?"

"i guess not."

"how was the wine?"

"not as good as it would have been if someone was here to share it with me."

"i'm sorry i missed it. i bought a bottle of beringer red at the corner liquor store so that i could have a glass while you had a glass back there in south dakota."

"you're kidding me."

"about what?"

"we both bought the same wine without knowing it!"

"get outta here :)."

"so about that dress."

"what dress?"

"the one you were going to wear yesterday."

"oh, right. it's deep blue, just above the knees. bare-backed with a scalloped neckline. lots of skin but tasteful. i would have worn my best pearls for you."

My mind played with the image I'd concocted of her: darkly toned exotic skin contrasted by the white luminosity of pearls; her hair thick and black, barely touching her temples.

"i've got a killer pair of black heels, almost nothing to them. sleek black hose. i would've knocked you over."

"sounds like you would have given me a heart attack."

"it's a certainty."

15

"what about you?"

"just plain old black lee's and a pressed green shirt, the last button open at the collar."

"a little casual for our first date, don't you think?"

"not when you consider i had on my best cheyenne outfitter's cowboy boots; buffalo hide uppers all polished up to a brilliant tan, shiny as a new penny."

"that'd be a little out of place at the restaurant i had in mind."

"i thought we were meeting at my place."

"wouldn't your wife take exception to that?"

A lump formed in my throat. I'd avoided discussing my marital status, though Roxanne knew I was married from my profile. I really didn't want to get into it. There was too much apprehension involved in facing reality.

"i guess she would."

"guess?"

"she would."

"i like to keep things honest and up front. if we're going to have any kind of relationship, cyber or otherwise, we need to be honest."

What a contradiction. By typing away like a fool on my keyboard to sustain an Internet rendezvous with a stranger I was robbing my family of my attention. By concealing my intense infatuation with Roxanne from Beth and allowing my feelings, as infantile as they were, to be expressed in writing to another woman, there was nothing close to honesty taking place.

"or otherwise?"

"let's just keep it here on the screen for now. we've got plenty of time for reality," Roxanne advised.

The click of the front door cylinder startled me. Ashamed that the potentiality of a real meeting, of a real relationship existed, I typed as rapidly as I could to avoid detection.

"gotta go."

"so soon?"

"yep. it's getting late."

"no time for a good night kiss?"

"<he leans in and kisses her tenderly on the forehead.>"

"that's not the kind of kiss i had in mind."

"sorry. it'll have to do for now."

"can i see you tomorrow night?"

"maybe friday. gotta go."

"<a tear falls slowly down her cheek, ruining her make-up>. ok."

Beth looked tired. Her significant green eyes were heavy, as heavy as the burden of the baby in her arms. Two large shopping bags hung ponderously from her wrists as she shuffled across the threshold. Our oldest daughter burst into the room, her clean white Scandinavian skin turning red from effort.

"Hi daddy," Anna shouted as she crossed the hard ceramic tiles of the foyer. With an energetic bound, she landed in my arms.

"What did you and mommy do?" I asked.

"We went shopping."

"Did you buy anything?"

"I got her a couple of new outfits," was Beth's plaintive response.

"You get anything for yourself?"

"We can't afford it. I picked up diapers and formula. I'm done trying to breast feed."

"Get down, sweetie. I'm gonna take the baby from mom."

My wife handed the sleeping infant to me as Anna released her stranglehold on my neck and dropped to the floor. In an instant, my oldest daughter disappeared up the stairs, shopping bags in tow, to try on her purchases.

"I'm going to take a hot bath," Beth said in a weary tone.

"Sure. I'll handle Jessie. She smells like she could use a change."

In the infant's room, just down the hall from ours, I sat cross-legged on the floor with my two-month-old daughter sleeping contentedly on the warm carpeting. Water coursed through the old pipes of our Victorian home behind a freshly painted plaster wall. I cleaned Jessie's butt and wrapped a small paper diaper around the thick pink skin of her waist. The odor and residual dust of Johnson's Baby Powder engulfed us. Cradling her precious form, I slipped her smallness beneath the blankets in her crib and turned off an overhead light.

Anna pranced out of her room just as I turned the corner. Though burdened by the guilt of confidential sin, I smiled at my older daughter. As I opened the door to the master bedroom, Anna darted by me, intent on finding her mother. I reached into the space and snatcher my daughter's lithe, pre-adolescent nine-year-old form off the floor and swung her over my shoulder.

"Time for bed."

"Ah dad, not now. I want to show mom my outfit."

"You can show her your outfit in the morning. It's after nine and you have school tomorrow."

"Read me a book."

"You get undressed and get your P.J.'s on and I'll read to you."

The girl sped away, working, as always, at peak RPM's.

Beth and I met in the center of our king-sized bed after *The Lorax* had saved the environment once again. Our lovemaking was tender and slow, the way it had always been. I felt content. I hoped she shared the emotion. I turned out the light, ignorant of my self-deception.

CHAPTER 3

Steady snow fell from low clouds hanging over the bluffs surrounding Rapid City. Christmas Eve service at Emmanuel Episcopal Church captured an insignificant portion of my attention. An acoustic guitar picked out a simple, melodic version of *Silent Night* as my wife, children, and I exited the building across rough stones. It was hard for me to concentrate on the day-to-day tasks of living, much less the complexities of Christian spirituality. I believed myself to be a Christian. I believed I loved God, loved Jesus, loved my marriage, my wife, and my kids, but there was something missing. I needed more.

I glanced at Beth, trim and radiant in her brown wool coat, her pale Norwegian complexion contrasting significantly with her green eyes. Her lips were pursed in an apprehensive smile as she greeted our friends and neighbors on our way out of the church. When I felt she was aware of my observation, my eyes diverted and fixed upon the back of Anna's blue velvet cloak. My daughter's blond hair, gathered tightly in a green ribbon with red accents, bounced gently off her neck as she walked next to her mom. Jessica squirmed in my arms, seeking attention.

"That was a lovely service."

"Yes it was."

"You seem distant, Mike. Is anything wrong?"

"No. I'm just tired."

"Christmas will do that to you."

I thought about Beth's family, her three brothers and two sisters and their spouses coming for dinner at our home tomorrow afternoon. Elmer and Gladys, Beth's parents, would not be there. They would not be anywhere. They had both died in a car accident shortly before Thanksgiving and were now sleeping peacefully in a cemetery in Bismarck, North Dakota. With the funeral and all, Beth hadn't been in any shape to celebrate

Thanksgiving. Christmas was going to be the first big family get together since the accident. She was the one that should have seemed distant and reflective.

Christmas with my in-laws had always been something special. Nana Betty, my maternal grandmother, raised me. I got dumped at her place in Sioux Falls when I was six. My old man ran off to who the hell knows where and my mom, Iris, couldn't keep sober long enough to take care of me, her only kid. There wasn't much Christmas for me growing up. Every year, Nana would put out her miniature aluminum tree no more than a foot high. That was the extent of the holiday decorating. She made sure I got a card and a ten-dollar bill. Nothing more, nothing less. The day after Christmas, the tree, little ornaments and all, went back into its original box until the next Christmas. Becoming part of Beth's family, being around her siblings, their significant others and kids for the holidays, was something special. With her parents' death, the task of keeping Christmas had fallen unkindly upon my wife's shoulders at a time when she didn't need anything additional complicating her life.

The girls were bundled tightly in their blankets and fast asleep when their new toys came out of the attic. There was no banter, no celebratory air about us as Beth and I pulled our daughters' unwrapped presents out of plastic Wal-Mart bags and arranged the gifts at the base of our Christmas tree.

"Anna's going to like this one," I commented softly, holding a new doll aloft in an attempt to stir some dialogue.

Elizabeth remained quiet, dutifully pulling presents from bags without acknowledging my observation. I placed the "Western-wear Barbie" complete with companion quarter horse, tack, Jeep, and horse trailer, next to a hand-stitched size 4 soccer ball.

"We went overboard," Beth mumbled.

"What?"

"We spent way too much this year."

"Why do you say that?"

"Because it's true."

I could tell from her voice that the issue wasn't what we had spent.

"Let's just have fun playing Santa," I urged.

There was no response. Beth continued to listlessly pull items out of the bags and place them absently under the boughs of the spruce tree.

"How about a glass of Tom and Jerry?"

"No thanks. I've got a lot of work to do tomorrow to get ready for my family. Maybe after we get through tomorrow I'll feel like a drink," my wife observed.

Beth looked past me. She focused her gaze on the shining lights of the Christmas tree, the first tree she had ever experienced without parents. I knew that thoughts of her mother and father were behind her melancholy. I just didn't know how to deal with them. A weak, crooked smile lightly touched her lips and vanished. She turned on her heels and climbed the stairs.

"I'll be up in a minute."

There was no response for a few seconds. Her delayed reply caused my heart to skip a beat.

"Don't stay up late on the Internet tonight, Mike. You can't keep coming to bed at all hours of the night, tossing and turning like you do. You're waking me up and I need my rest."

There it was. She knew that I was on the computer late. Though there was no evidence that she knew why I was up long into the night on the Internet, it really didn't matter. It was obvious from the tremor in her voice, an abnormal hesitancy I'd not heard before, that she was concerned about me. Or was it that she was concerned for herself? Or us?

"I'm just doing some last minute research on the IRS website. I'll be right up."

"For Chrissake, Mike, it's Christmas Eve. Can't it wait for a couple of days?"

"It'll just be a few minutes."

"Fine."

It was obvious from the inflection in her voice that it was anything but "fine".

"i can't stay up too long. it's christmas eve, you know."

"really? i must have missed all of the three billion television and newspaper ads reminding me."

"hey rox, ease up will you?"

We'd developed a casual, friendly diction to our writing. We were like two life-long friends in our speech and interaction. That the closeness had evolved over the span of less than a month was amazing to me. Was I that lonely? That needy? Despite all of the love and happiness surrounding my life?

"why should i ease up?"

"because it's christmas."

"oh yeah. i remember. that's where everyone in school, regardless of your religion, has to sing christmas songs."

"well, you could run away from the 'dark side' and join us, you know."

"mmm. let me think. cast my fate with a guy who, though proclaimed king and the son of god, ended up being skewered by a roman spear, hung up on a cross with thieves and killed? you'll have to be more convincing."

"i'll work on that. i think beth is getting tired of this."

"tired of what?"

"us."

"does she know there is an 'us'?"

"not really. but she's not too happy i'm spending all this time on the computer."

"just a question."

"what?"

"is there an 'us'?"

"what do you mean?"

"you know what i mean. are we more than a couple of strange people living out a fantasy that has no meaning, no substance?"

"we're both real, aren't we?" I asked.

There was a significant delay in Roxanne's response. I felt her mind searching, trying, as I was, to sort out what our late-night rendezvous meant, if anything.

"we're real. i'm flesh and blood. i expect you are too."

"so what more do we need than that, the knowledge we are?"

"mike, you're turning this into a story from the *velveteen rabbit.*"

"lol. what did you get for hannakah?"

"a new negligee from samuel, among other things. want to see?"

"describe it."

"i can't-it's too revealing. you'll just have to use your imagination."

"how can I do that when I don't even know what you look like?"

"well, i'm five foot seven, long thick black hair. a little gray here and there but i cover it up pretty well. an energetic three-year-old will do that to ya."

"sounds wonderful so far. tell me more."

"i'm between 125 and 135, depending on the time of the month."

"that's more information than i need to know."

"the fact i have a cycle is a surprise to you?"

"like i said, too much information."

"i've got a nice figure. dark complexion. deep brown eyes-really, they're almost black. a great rack!"

"what did you say?"

"you heard me. i'm not repeating myself. your turn."

23

"well, i'm six foot, 179. blue eyes. really almost gray. blond hair, short. i'm in pretty good shape-work out three or four times a week. my friends say I look like jeff bridges."

"you sound very handsome. do you have a gif?"

"no. but maybe soon. how about you?"

"nope. i'm too afraid some crazy person will figure out a way to break into my hard drive and steal my identity. you know, I do live in canada, the great wilderness. guys up here have been known to get desperate."

"so I guess we'll just have use our imaginations for the time being."

"looks like it. well, i hear sam coming up the walk."

"this time of night?"

"he's on call."

"what's he do?"

"he's a doctor."

"two professionals in the house?"

"yep. i scored higher on the mcats but went to law school instead."

"i bet you don't let him forget that fact."

"you got that right. <places her hand on his shoulder and moves his free hand to her hip. with a tenuous motion, she presses her warm body against him and lets a deep french kiss linger in his mouth.>"

"goodnight, michael."

My message to her came back undelivered. She was no longer on line. The house had become cold. My half-consumed Tom and Jerry sat in a mug on an old table serving as my computer desk. Rather than wake Beth, I curled up beneath the thick wool of an antique comforter and slept fitfully on the couch.

CHAPTER 4

My desk at work was stacked high with the financial records of St. Vincent's Nursing Home. Three flights up from the street, perched above the despair of winter on the Plains, I drank black coffee out of a thick porcelain mug. Light haze cloaked the sun's authority, muting the intensity of the day. I stared vacantly out a window.

Beth and I were having trouble. Christmas turned out to be a morose, dismal affair. We would have been better to visit "Embalming World" than have her siblings over to celebrate the birth of Jesus. All the women did was cry. Beth's two sisters and her two sisters-in-law spent the whole time bawling. All the men did was drink. With all the crying and drinking, the consummation of our upset was a brutal, knockdown, drag-out fistfight between Beth's older brother Roger and me.

Roger's always been an asshole. He was one before Beth's parents died. He'll likely be one after he himself dies if that's possible. He made some crack about Beth having such an easy, good life, as if the deaths of their parents shouldn't affect her, as if somehow her grief couldn't be real. Because of Roger's past, I could kind of see his perspective.

He's gone through three terrible marriages, screwed up his kids so bad that they aren't allowed to see him anymore and has been through chemical dependency "spin dry" at least twice with no success. He probably does need his parents more than my wife does. It's become pretty clear to me that Roger will never grow up on his own.

I would've ignored him if kept his mouth shut. But when my brother-in-law staggered into the kitchen and bitched at Beth about her turkey dressing not being the same as their mom's, punctuating his point by dropping the entire serving bowl of giblets and bread into the garbage, Roger crossed a line. I grabbed him from behind and tried to ride him out of the kitchen, onto the back porch, and out of the house.

The old drunk fought back. He caught me square on the chin with a left, then landed a right to my right eye before David, his "little" brother (younger but appreciably bigger) helped me bull-dog Roger out the back door. The three of us fell off the porch, busting through a redwood railing in the process, and landed four feet below in fresh snow. That was the last I saw of Roger on Christmas.

All of the commotion upset the women. But not Beth's brother Tom. Tom was the only male in the house who avoided the fracas. Uncle Tom, the quiet one, the studious one, watched *A Muppet Christmas Carol* with the kids in the living room as adult insanity swirled about them.

"What the hell got into you?" Beth asked between tears as David and I limped back into the house covered with snow.

"Mike needed some help," Dave replied through a sheepish grin.

"That's your brother you just tossed out into the cold."

"He's a jerk. He deserves to have his ass kicked. I'm glad I was the one to do it."

"Chrissakes. It's fucking Christmas," my wife moaned.

I tried to calm her. The turmoil was too great. The food was ruined. The mood was ruined. The day was ruined. Even the innocence of the children was ruined.

The phone rang. I'd just finished lunch. It was my first day back in the office after the holidays and I was trying to stay awake while studying a distant hillside through the dirty glass of a window.

"Michael. Is that you?"

The voice was unfamiliar, the accent foreign yet reminiscent of something obvious, something well known.

"Yes. Who is this?"

There was an excruciating pause.

"Roxanne."

I detected a strong heritage of Canada in the pronunciation of her name.

"You're kidding me."

"Nope. It's me. Surprised?"

I was stunned. I hadn't given her my last name, my phone number, or the name of my employer. How had she tracked me down?

"How did you find me?"

"Find you? I didn't know you were lost."

"You know what I mean."

My heart was racing. I felt an urgency that I hadn't felt since leaning close to Beth to kiss her for the first time so very long ago. My mouth went dry. Logic seemed impossible to harness.

"There are only four accountants in Rapid City named Michael. Only one is a member of the Black Hills Writer's Circle."

Resourceful. I had to admit she was damned resourceful.

"I went to the Waverly Branch of the Thunder Bay Public Library and looked up accountants in Rapid City. I found the four names. Then I went on line and found the Writer's Circle Website. You were the only Michael on both lists. By the way, I loved the short story."

"Which one?"

"*An Artist's Lament.* That brought back a lot of memories."

"How so?"

"I had a boyfriend who was a painter. I was a shit to him. I could really empathize with the male character in your story. I wish I'd have known then what I know now."

27

Don't we all, I thought.

Her voice, the way she curled her tongue around vowels, elongating them, emphasizing them, aroused me, causing me to feel exhilaration and shame in equal measure.

"Where are you calling from?"

"Work. I have a calling card."

"Won't they get on you for racking up a long distance bill that's not work related?"

"The calling card is a personal account."

"Won't your husband wonder why you're calling South Dakota?"

"He doesn't pay any attention to my bills. We have separate checking accounts; he pays his, along with the household bills, and I pay mine."

"I'm amazed."

"At what?"

"That you could find me-that you would call me."

"Shouldn't I have? I can hang up. We can forget this ever happened."

"That's not what I mean. I'm happy you called. It's just so..."

"Weird? I know. I thought the same thing."

I paused for a moment.

"Your accent reminds me of Ireland," I mused.

"Ireland?"

"Yep. Like in the movie *Angela's Ashes*."

"That's an interesting observation since I'm a Canadian Jew."

"I know. But you still sound Irish."

My secretary Jill buzzed me on the intercom.

"Roxanne, just a second. I gotta answer a page."

I clicked on the intercom button.

"What's up?"

"Your wife called to remind you to pick up Anna at school on your way home."

"Thanks a lot, Jill."

"You're welcome, Mike."

28

I turned off the speaker.

"Roxanne? You still there?"

"Still here. Guess what I'm wearing today."

We were headed into dangerous territory. Common sense dictated that I should tell the woman on the other end of the phone, a woman I'd never met but had spent hours with, to the detriment of my marriage and my peace of mind, to never call me again. That's what a strong person would have done. I found out that I'm not that strong.

"What?"

"A light gray two piece business suit. Very conservative. Smokey gray nylons that end...Well, I'll leave the rest of the description to your vivid imagination."

I took a deep breath.

"They're held up by garters. Silver in color, all delicate lace and silk."

I wanted her to say more, to continue describing her intimate attire, to reveal what else she was wearing. A fever raged within me as I sat in my office, desperate to stop myself from perpetuating insanity, all the while hoping she'd tantalize me with additional details.

"I don't know what to say."

"I wore them just for you. Do you like them?"

"Why are you doing this?"

"Doing what?"

"Calling me at work, telling me these things? What good can come of it?"

There was a terse interruption in our conversation. I thought she had hung up.

"Maybe this was a bad idea."

"I didn't say that. I'm just surprised to hear from you."

"Good surprised or bad surprised?"

I took a deep breath.

"Good surprised," I admitted.

"I'm not crazy, you know. I thought you and I were building some kind of connection, that you wanted to hear from the real me. Typing words across a computer screen seems to me to be pretty childish and crass."

"I like hearing from the real you. I'm sorry I upset you. You can call me here anytime you want."

"Do you want to call me? You can get me on my cell phone. I usually have it with me when I'm at work."

"Sure. Give me the number. I don't have a calling card so I'll have to figure out some way to do this."

"You can use my calling card number. I'll give it to you," she responded.

As I accepted the new parameters of our relationship, a deep wave of regret assaulted my soul. But the buttressing effect of knowing another woman cared for me, wanted me, longed to talk to me, momentarily bested my ascending guilt.

CHAPTER 5

"Mike, what's wrong? You don't seem yourself?"

Albert Lucan, an old buddy from high school and the one person on the planet besides Beth that knows me, really knows me, asked the question as we shot hoops in the driveway of his place out to the west of town. Spring had arrived in full force, melting the heavy snow of winter, leaving the cracked asphalt of Al's driveway clear and dry. Small snowdrifts, hard packed due to sun and age, remained beneath the eaves of the house and the garage, and under the thick branches of ornamental yews lining the front sidewalk of Al's suburban rambler. An aroma of barbecue, the fragrance of charcoal burning, wafted over us, carried on a slight breeze from the backyard, where a rust-stained Weber grill sought to contain the heat of smoldering fuel.

"Just overly tired," I replied.

My shot from behind the three-point line, a crude white stripe hand-painted across the battered surface of the driveway, fell a foot short of the backboard. Al, considerably taller than me at six four and appreciably more athletic, swooped in, his bald head shining in the high sun, and slammed the ball through the netting with grace.

I picked up my can of Schmidt, a sportsman container bearing the likeness of a walleye leaping out of a Minnesota lake, and sucked down the last of the flat beer. Al set up ten feet from the portable Plexiglas basketball backboard. The contraption was mounted on curiously cheap plastic wheels. My companion deftly lobbed the ball towards the hole. Nothing but net.

"Nice shot."

"Practice. You sure nothing's bothering you buddy? You seem awfully quiet."

I am a talker. Al generally let me do the gabbing around the girls in high school and later on, at college in Brookings, where we both attended South Dakota State.

31

We're both over thirty and still married to our college sweethearts.

"Hey Debra Jo," Lucan said lightly as he retrieved the ball from behind a pile of split oak, the wood dried and ready for the fireplace. A dark haired little girl, diminutive and shy, peeked at us through a gap underneath the cedar fence surrounding the backyard deck.

A high-pitched giggle was the girl's only response.

"I'm gonna get you."

Al crouched low to the ground, positioning himself eye to eye with his daughter. A squeal of laughter and the sound of tiny feet scurrying away emanated from behind the heavy boards of the fence.

"She's quite a little girl," I noted.

"A miracle," Al replied wistfully.

My friend's reference to his daughter's precarious existence was not meant to be casual. I knew that Al and his wife Trish had gone to hell and back with Debra Jo, their only child.

Debra had been born with a significant defect in her heart. Something about one of the chambers being so porous that any blood pumped into it merely slopped back to its place of origin. Debbie had required seven complex, expensive surgeries at St. Mary's Hospital in Rochester, at the hands of surgeons and specialists from the Mayo Clinic, before her second birthday. Here she was, nearly seven, lithe and quick, bearing no restrictions beyond some innocuous medications, darting like a demon across the lawn after my oldest daughter, Anna.

"She's gonna try soccer this year."

"Think that's wise?"

"You sound like Trish. Christ, Mike, she's a kid. The doc's say she's all right to go. Her stamina is where it should be. She's quick as hell. There's no reason she can't at least try to live a normal life."

I nodded. Al's gaze followed the frenzied pace of his little girl across the greening grass of the yard. Noting Al's thickening body and absent hair, I recalled the sleek athlete my friend had once been at SDSU, where he set a single game scoring record by putting in 48 points against Valley City. Now he was a dad. He knew his own child best.

I retrieved the ball and put up one last toss. As the well-worn rubber of the street ball left my hand, an image of Roxanne, her dark eyes covered with Ray Ban sunglasses, her neck exposed and supple, floated to me across the warm prairie air.

She'd sent me a photograph. By snail mail, in an envelope marked "Personal". It arrived in my office a month ago. Her picture was buried in the bowels of my workstation, at the bottom of one of the drawers in my desk, hidden from prying eyes.

I found it difficult to preclude her smile, to relegate her existence to mere fantasy. I knew that my heart was confused. My mind was perplexed to such a degree that my best friend could see the anxiety, the inner debate, etched upon my face as we played a casual game of "Horse".

My jump shot banked sharply off the glass and fell through the nylon netting as Al and I left the driveway and followed his little girl into the back yard.

CHAPTER 6

"how's it going?"

I hadn't heard from Roxanne in awhile. There wasn't any particular reason for the interruption other than the fact that we both had families, jobs, and reality to contend with.

"not so bad. have i done something wrong?" I asked, not certain at the time that her silence and our lack of communication over a rather lengthy time frame was innocent.

"nope. just darn busy. i had a jury trial that went a week long."

"how'd you do?"

"i kicked the plaintiff's ass."

"i expect you're pretty tough in a courtroom."

"you got that straight, eh?"

"what kind of case was it?"

"just a run of the mill traffic accident. but the guy claiming injury was overreaching. i'd offered him a good settlement, fifteen thousand canadian, for a soft tissue neck injury. his lawyer convinced him to go to trial. thunder bay jurors aren't like toronto folks. we don't raise fools up here."

"you still sound fired up about the case."

"why don't you cool me off?"

"how's that?"

"a nice shower might be just what the doctor ordered to cool me down."

There it was again. Tempting coyness. Something that had been part of my courting of Beth but had disappeared in the routine of our daily life together.

"you can take a shower anytime you want to. you don't need my help."

"but we can save water this way. show the world we're ecologically minded."

I hadn't received a phone call from her for a month. It was October. Summer in the Black Hills had passed. Early fall clung to the hillside, slowly changing the leaves to color. It was a Saturday afternoon. My daughters and my wife were at a church rummage sale helping to sort out and label clothes. I'd stayed behind with the promise that I'd clean the garage and arrange our cross-country and downhill skiing gear for the upcoming winter. The task included hoisting our bikes and golf clubs into the loft of the garage in preparation for the first snowfall. The first snow would signal the end of autumn and the beginning of another long winter in the Black Hills.

"i've got something to tell you," I scrawled.

"what's that?", she wrote.

There was a slight delay in her response, as if she was apprehensive.

"thunder bay is how far from grand marais?" I asked.

"a little over an hour. why?"

"i'm coming up there right after thanksgiving, american thanksgiving that is, to audit the books of the cook county medical center."

There was a gap in our written conversation. A familiar feeling of guilt crept over my consciousness as I awaited her reply. Despite a lingering measure of sameness, of acceptance of things the way they were, Beth and I didn't have, so far as I could pinpoint, any serious difficulties in our marriage.

By providing information about my trip to Minnesota's North Shore to Roxanne Epstein, a person I had never met, I was placing my marriage, Beth's blind trust in me, on the line. For what? Sensual attraction? Mystery? A cold chill slid down my spine, causing me to reach for the power button on the notebook computer.

"i'd like to see you," she wrote.

Her response flew across the telephone wires from Canada to Rapid City, emerging just as the tip of my index finger touched the soft plastic of the shut off switch. My brain raced, seeking an easy way out, out of the complexities of beginning a relationship with a person I knew only through voice, through stolen moments on the computer, and through a single photograph; a portrait treasured and secreted in my desk. Hesitancy overwhelmed intrigue; compassion for my wife, the mother of my two children, respect for her faith in me surged across the furthest reaches of my mind. Almost as if in a dream, a trance induced by wanton sensuality and desire, I began to type:

"i'll be staying at lutsen. at the eagle ridge condominiums. from monday morning until thursday morning. the last week of the month."

"alone?"

A reasonable question.

"yes."

"do you want me to come down?"

I felt blood run out my brain. My right hand remained suspended above the keys. Thoughts rummaged through my mind, details soared in flights of fancy, bumping headlong into bits and pieces of dread.

"that would be nice."

"nice. that word really sucks. how about wonderful, exciting, intoxicating? nice. for a writer, you really do have a terrible way with the english language."

She was right. If I was going to take the step, make an attempt to meet her, see her, using junior high grammar wasn't the way to win her over. Instead of dwelling on my deficiencies as a scribe, I changed the subject.

"do you ski?"

"that's an interesting switch."

"i hear lutsen is the best place in the midwest next to terry peak to ski."

"if you're talking downhill, we've got some nice hills right here in town, but none of them are as breath-taking or as long as lutsen," she wrote. "where's terry peak?" she asked.

36

"about an hour from here. it's pretty substantial, over a thousand vertical, but the snow is iffy at times."

"that would beat the pants off anything around here. but there's never any problem with snow at lutsen. is my offer making you nervous?"

"what offer?"

"to meet."

Of course it made me nervous. Sweat rolled down my underarms, dampening my plaid flannel shirt. I struggled to understand my need; my desperate longing for a woman I'd never met in the flesh. As that singular word cascaded through the tunnels of my understanding, I knew it was a mistake. Flesh. Thinking in terms of flesh was demeaning, it minimized what we'd shared, even if others would come to view our connection as trite flirtation; even if Beth might some day come to the conclusion that I was no longer worthy of love.

"i'll admit that i'm a little conflicted."

"it doesn't have to be more than you want it to be. i'm willing to go at whatever pace makes you comfortable," she offered.

The Canadian woman wasn't pushing me into something I didn't want, that I was incapable of understanding. I deflected her offer.

"you never answered my question."

"which one?"

"do you ski?"

"both cross-country and downhill. i raced downhill for the junior nationals when I was a kid," Roxanne disclosed.

I closed my eyes and tried to envision a teenaged version of Rox, dressed in brilliant yellow or blue Lycra, her hair compressed tightly under the plastic of a racing helmet, waiting to run the gates at Vail or Aspen.

"were you good?"

"until i blew out my left knee. i took a header at whistler when i was sixteen. at the time i was ranked fourth in my age group in canada. tried to come back from a complete acl reconstruction but my confidence was gone."

"i'm not sure you'll want to ski with me. i'm no expert. My biggest claim to fame is a bronze medal in the terry peak nastar race last year."

"i think we'll do just fine. i can always give you some private lessons.:)."

"roxanne?"

"yes?"

"i want to meet you but can we take it slow?"

"the slower the better, mr. accountant, the slower the better. gotta go. think about it. i'm not interested in going any place you don't want to go on your own."

My message to her came back. She had left the Net, returning to reality, leaving me to unravel my feelings and to determine which road I was willing to travel.

CHAPTER 7

A leaf fell in our backyard. I watched the dead vegetation descend until captured by a draft from the west, from somewhere out on the Great Plains. The wind changed the path of the leaf's flight and caused the decaying remnant to soar.

Beth reclined next to me in bed; her breathing creating a steady, sad pattern to her slumber. My wife wasn't dreaming, so far as I could tell. I had been. I had been dreaming of making love to a woman. Her name was Roxanne. I was ashamed.

My head rested heavily on the smooth fabric of my pillow. I followed the ascent of the oak leaf until it disappeared. My wife of ten years whispered something. I couldn't make out the words. Her hair was tangled around her head, covering most of her face. I knew her eyes contained miraculous pools of emerald. I thought back to when we first met as freshmen at SDSU in Brookings. How she was so much quicker, so much smarter than me. How her skin tanned so easily in the heat of the sun. How her breasts rose and fell when she napped on a lounge chair next to the pool on South Padre Island where we went for Spring Break during our senior year.

All of those moments, including the moments of pain and degradation Beth endured giving birth to our two daughters, assailed me. There was no reason, no lack of love, no failure to connect between us, which compelled my infatuation with another woman. There was only a sense of thrill, an urgency to explore driving me; surely an insufficient basis upon which to risk the life I'd chosen, the life Beth and I had made.

"When will you be back?" she asked later that morning.

My wife's voice caught me in mid-thought. I was attempting to categorize and isolate my feelings for the other woman as I exited the shower. Beth was standing in her expensive pajamas, her breasts naturally coaxed towards the floor, the contours of her bosom revealed by gaps in her nightshirt where the buttons wouldn't hold the two halves of the silk garment together.

"Thursday night. It's a long drive. I'll start in the morning around five. I should be able to make it in one day."

"What car are you taking?"

Her voice was unconcerned. There was no evidence she suspected what I was about to do.

"The Jeep. Four wheel drive might come in handy."

"That's fine. The van has front wheel drive which is all I'll probably need around here."

She leaned against the archway. I stood in front of a vanity mirror, the glass clouded with steam, drops of water sliding down my naked back, trying to shave. I wanted to be done with the task, to leave my life, my family, and my past behind. Not permanently. Just for an instant, for a snapshot in time.

"You're putting on a little weight," Beth noted.

There was ample evidence to support her comment. I'd gained twenty-five pounds in the span of four months. A small pouch of skin was beginning to form around my waistline. The added weight was nearly undetectable when I was fully clothed. Beth's remark stung. I didn't let her see my anger. I wasn't about to give her a reason to suspect I was becoming unbalanced, unglued.

"Guess so. Guess I need to go on a diet."

"I kind of like it. Makes you look distinguished."

"I don't feel distinguished. More like stuffed, like a baked potato. I need to get more exercise."

I packed my battered Samsonite suitcase without further conversation. Beth left our room. I could hear her walking through the main floor of the house, picking up dirty dishes and abandoned toys. Our eyes met again when I entered the kitchen in search of breakfast.

"Is something bothering you?" she asked, standing in front of the kitchen sink, watching a sudden rain squall roll across the lawn towards the house. "You seem distant."

"Just a lot of work to do and a long drive to do it."

"They should fly you at least to the Cities, if not Duluth."

"The mileage checks are what pay for our cars, remember? Besides, I'd rather drive. At least then I know who's behind the wheel."

My teeth bit down hard on shredded wheat. I swallowed the grainy food in clumps. Beth filled my travel mug with hot coffee and accompanied me to the front door, her hair straight and dirty from sleep, her skin blotched and unpainted, natural against the artificial light of a chandelier in the foyer. Outside, our red Cherokee, its metal skin glistening from the passing rain, stood next to the curb waiting for a driver.

"Take your time."

There was just a hint of sadness to my wife's voice. I drew her body in and hugged her. My heart was heavy as I stepped across the threshold and out into the wet air.

CHAPTER 8

Brazen waves crashed against ancient rocks. White foam pounded the thick boulders of the North Shore of Lake Superior. I sat on cold stone, my ski parka buttoned tight against the day's fury, studying the inland sea, contemplating my place in the universe.

I'd spent Tuesday working non-stop with the hospital staff in Grand Marais to prepare their books and records for a federal Medicare Audit that was going to take place after the first of the year.

"Michael, are we still on for tomorrow?"

Roxanne's voice had been oddly comforting. Despite the fact that her existence was the root cause of inner turmoil, there was something strangely soothing about her diction, about the pattern of her speech, about the way she said my name.

Silence ensued. I wanted to say "yes". I knew I should respond "no". My conflict was resolved by yielding to selfishness:

"Yes."

Another pause.

"Should I guess where you'll be or do you actually want to set something up so we can find each other?"

"I'll meet you at the Bluefin Bay for breakfast. Know where it is?"

"I pass it fifty times a year on my way down the Shore. Of course I know where it is. What time?"

"How about 7:30?"

"Make it 8:00. It's a long drive from here."

Austere light broke through the high clouds rolling across the lake. I left the lakeshore and entered the café. I was alone. My eyes were uneasily focused on the restaurant parking lot as I waited for Roxanne to arrive. I knew she'd be driving a yellow Eagle Talon, a car that would be tough to miss. A nervous chill occupied my bones. As I considered the moment, my body began to shake.

It was nearly 8:30. There was no sign of her. I was about to give up and drive to Lutsen for a day of skiing on my own when a bright yellow coupe emerged from a heavy cloud of steam that had come off Lake Superior and stalled above the highway.

My mind raced. It was too late to leave, too late in the game to pack it in.

Should I stand up from the table and walk to the door to greet her? Should I go outside and open the driver's door of her car? I thought. *There's no protocol, so far as I'm aware, applicable to a first meeting with your Internet mistress,* I silently mused.

"Hi. I'm Mike," I said as I approached her car.

Roxanne left her ski gloves on the front seat of the Talon and exited the vehicle with grace. She was tall, exactly the height she claimed to be. She was also striking. I extended my bare hand, its flesh lifeless and pale in the uneven light.

"I'm Roxanne. Pleased to meet you Michael. It's cold out here. Let's go in and warm up," she said, closing the driver's door to the coupe with a shove.

Her skin was naturally dark. Her lips were full and accented by lipstick. She was dressed for downhill skiing in bright green warm-ups, a matching jacket cut short below the waist, a yellow knitted ski hat, and Mukluks.

At the top of Moose Mountain, she stepped into her Marker bindings and positioned her Elans at the apex of the slope. Her gloved hands seemed delicate, her fingers long and spidery, as she drew them through the loops of her ski poles. She stood patiently, her breath creating little clouds of moisture in the damp air, as she waited for me.

She twisted and pounced across mounds of frozen snow like a professional ski racer making her way through slalom gates. I pushed myself hard, trying to keep up. Half way into the moguls, my left ski tip caught an ice patch, sending me head over heels down the slope. I came to rest next to Roxanne. She looked down at me with a wry smile:

"Like I said. Maybe you could stand a few private lessons."

CHAPTER 9

Amy Maddox, a folk singer I'd never heard of, occupied the small stage in the Lutsen Mountain Bar. Roxanne sat next to me surveying the crowd through ebony eyes. Her neon jacket hung loosely from the back of her chair; a tall, narrow stool, perched on thin wrought iron legs. The skier's hands, the dark skin of her fingers reflecting her birth color and not the artificial results of a tanning booth, grasped the stem of a plastic wineglass. Red wine filled the carafe on the table in front of her. The liquid in the decanter vibrated to the beat of the music.

I tried to concentrate on the singer. I riveted my attention on Ms. Maddox. The artisan played a battered 6-string and sang a love song she'd written. Her voice was sweet and clear. Her words were prophetic and agonizing.

"She's good," my companion whispered.

Roxanne looked at me with steady regard. If she was wracked with misgivings about the evening, it didn't show.

"No, she's very good," I offered in correction. "Her words mesh perfectly with the tune."

"I thought you were a rock and roll fan."

Roxanne's gaze caused me to blush.

"That doesn't mean I can't enjoy an artist in another genre."

"Touché'."

My legs quivered. I was uncertain if the reflex was due to nerves or the pace that we'd set skiing down the mountain. I was unfamiliar with the hill. My Jewish friend from Canada had been my tour guide, taking me to little-used, out-of-the-way trails. On icy, narrow paths through trees, she taught me to "short swing"; an archaic and little used technique for negotiating tight, dangerous slopes. I was exhausted.

"I got a room at the Lodge," she continued.

"That wasn't necessary."

"I thought it was. I didn't know what might happen. It's for the best. This way, Sam can call me and know that I'm alone, that I'm safe. I told him I was in the States taking depositions."

Roxanne didn't smile. I raised my drink glass to my chapped lips and pulled heavily on a rum and coke. One more drink and I'd be ready to talk about more serious matters, maybe address the ultimate, unspoken question lingering between us.

Ms. Maddox took a break. Someone behind the bar turned up the lights so the patrons could see each other and engage in conversation without squinting. Beyond the picture windows facing the hill, the steep incline of Hari-Kari and Koo-Koo, Lutsen's expert runs, climbed towards the summit. Sparse lighting revealed moments of shadow across the face of Hari-Kari where moguls pockmarked the run. Ice had formed in the recesses of the bumps; ice that would be there to test skiers tomorrow.

"Are you sure you want to do this?"

Her question contained compassion. I felt a wave of apprehension crest.

"I'm sure."

"It's been a wonderful day, Mike. There's no need for anything else to happen if you don't want it to. I'm perfectly happy hanging out and drinking wine with you."

"There've gotta be loads of folks back in Thunder Bay who know you much better than I do, people that you'd rather hang out with."

The instant I said the words, I knew that they would sting. My face must have telegraphed some aspect of premonition. She ignored my insensitivity.

"I don't have anyone, not even Sam, that I can talk to like I talk to you. He's my husband, the father of my son. I love him, love him in the unique and special way that can only be given by a wife to her husband. But he's

46

49 years old. There's an angst, a heartache deep inside him, maybe the result of being Jewish and isolated in a small city in the middle of nowhere, away from his family, that I just don't understand."

"But you're Jewish. Doesn't that help?"

She sighed and sipped deeply of the wine.

"I converted just before Alexander was born. My mom's Polish, my dad's half-Serbian and half-Croatian. I was raised Roman Catholic. There are only a handful of Jewish families in Thunder Bay. They've been there for so long, they're all assimilated into the Anglo culture. Sam came from Toronto, where his family is well established, where their religion is more vibrant. Thunder Bay is, for all intents and purposes, like the end of the earth for someone like Samuel."

"Why does he stay?"

The singer climbed back onto the stage. A female bartender found the dimmer switch and plunged the place into darkness. Another song, quicker in pace, flew off the guitarist's instrument.

"He's the best neurosurgeon in Thunder Bay. Even with government-run health care, he makes more money staying where he is than he'd ever make back east. Plus, despite the isolation, Thunder Bay is a wonderful place to raise a family. There's the symphony, museums, a great library, and plenty of downhill and cross country skiing to keep me sane during the unrelenting depths of winter."

It seemed like the appropriate time. The fingers of my right hand extracted a neatly folded sheet of paper from the back pocket of my trousers. I handed the document to Roxanne.

"What's this?" she asked.

"Something I wrote for you."

"You're so damn sweet," she sighed, looking away from my eyes, trying to hide her reaction. She opened the paper carefully, smoothing the edges flat with long, narrow fingers. I watched her expression as she began to read:

A Kiss is Just A Kiss...Until

It doesn't matter who she really is, who I really am, or where this all will lead. It doesn't matter that we both have children, that we live separate lives, that the geographic distance between us incorporates impassable rivers, snow-covered mountain ranges, and millions of acres of forest. All that matters is, in this complex, rapidly failing world, she and I together, if only for brief interludes in fantasy time, share hope.

There are no physical expectations or parameters imposed. I do not wince at the latest color of her hair. I do not notice the fact that she may have put on a few pounds since we last spoke. I do not criticize her choice of coffee or her choice of friends.

She, in turn, does not care if I wear the same blue jeans two days in a row. She does not find fault with the blasting volume of Jude Cole in the background as we talk. She is unconcerned when I tell her that I spend time with others, talking in the dark through my fingertips and my keyboard, just as I talk to her. None of these mundane, ordinary items matter in the extraordinary world our friendship occupies.

At times, our voices mesh, our minds click, and we discuss things in harmonious order. We do not always agree, but often, our dialogue manages to cross the country in electronic perfection. Other times, just like in real life, we miss each other's intent; misconstrue each other's message. But unlike the real world, unlike a conversation between a man and a woman in a crowded bar, there is no cultural barrier to real communication. We are, for the greatest part, open and honest about errors in our perceptions. We tell each other what we think, what we want, what we need. And we go on.

Our affection for each other is genuine. Our respect for each other, I believe, is even greater. Passion can be felt simmering just beneath the surface of our words. It is not, however, passion which compels us to seek each other in the darkness of night. We do not search for each other out of pleasure, though there is infinite pleasure in our relationship, in our fleeting encounters. We look for each other in hopes of continuing to understand our own selves, who we are, why we feel lonely and isolated in a world crowded with friends, family, and business associates.

At times we kiss. While our lips embrace as mere symbols on our respective monitor screens, the embrace of our souls is no illusion. It is real. It has consequences. For us, for our loved ones, for the world.

When we part, hearts racing, minds tumbling in an emotional circus of imagination and possibilities, we cannot sleep. Our partners wake and ask us why we are tossing and turning long into the night. We dare not answer them. We dare not think too deeply about what it is we have or why we go to such great lengths to protect a love that others call mere illusion.

Mike.

"It's beautiful. Thank you for the sentiment. Thank you for being you," she whispered, placing the palm of her hand, her skin moist, on my left wrist.

I ordered another drink. Roxanne sipped slowly on a second glass of wine. I felt a sudden surge of emotion. A fragment of cologne floated by. The mix of Roxanne and perfume dredged up primeval desires that I thought I was going to be able to suppress.

She slipped beneath the dry sheets of my bed. I left the blinds on the windows open. A blazing quarter moon rose across the snowfields of Moose Mountain. My hands shook as I moved to touch the bare skin of her back. She snuggled next to me. She faced away from me, averting her eyes. Her legs and bottom were nestled against me.

"Michael, if you're anxious about this because you think I'll be after you for something permanent, that's not why I'm here."

My fingers rested on her hipbones. Smooth skin greeted my touch. I found it difficult to maintain my normal breathing pattern.

"What do you mean?"

"I don't know how to explain this any other way than directly. I'm 29 years old. I'll likely be married to Samuel for the rest of my life. It's not that I want to hurt him, to destroy what he and I have built."

"Than what is it?"

There was a slight whimper to her voice as she answered:

"I just need to be held, to be wanted, by someone who's not obligated to me. You're a wonderful man. An honest man. That's why I'm here."

A cloud passed across the face of the partial moon. I moved closer. Our bodies became completely immersed in each other.

"Why are you here?" she asked.

Her inquiry caught me off guard. Not that I hadn't asked the question a hundred times during the drive from Rapid City to the North Shore of Lake Superior. All of the responses I'd dredged up; lust, self-gratification, ego, envy, and curiosity seemed cheap and insubstantial in the face of what we were about to embark upon.

"I'm here because of you."

It was the best answer I could come up with under the weight of immediacy.

"Do you love me?"

A dangerous question from a woman who'd just confessed that she'd never leave her husband.

"Yes."

My answer leaked out from between my lips. There was no thought, no rational debate with myself before I responded. The word simply escaped, as natural as carbon dioxide being expelled after a breath.

"I love you too," she admitted.

My hands slid up the sides of her body. It was silent, so silent that the beating of our hearts could be heard echoing within the closeness of the rented room.

CHAPTER 10

She was in the shower. Vague light formed a silhouette of her body. Water pounded her back. Her face was turned towards the wall. She held herself in grief. Waves of upset caused her slender form to shudder as the shower attacked her body. Her hand reached for a bar of soap. I averted my eyes to allow her privacy, convinced that we had made a terrible mistake.

I stared at the clock radio. It was after midnight. I hadn't called Beth. I wasn't about to call her now. Whatever lies I was going to sell could wait until morning. I'd be back in the car, driving towards Rapid City, at first light. Maybe I wouldn't call at all. Maybe I would just push the pedal to the floor and try to outrun my sin.

"How are you feeling?" I asked as she stepped out of the bathroom.

A white bath towel covered her torso. Small drops of water remained suspended in her hair. Beads of moisture clung to the exposed skin of her shoulders and upper arms.

"Not so good."

"I'm sorry."

"Don't apologize. I knew what I was getting into when I came here."

"Was it..." my words were cut short by her anticipation of my question.

"You were fine. It has nothing to do with the sex. Trust me, you did your part."

I knew better than to try to assuage her regret. For some reason, I couldn't keep my mouth shut.

"Then what?"

She sat down on the edge of the bed. The skin of her face glistened. She was more attractive in grief than she had been when we sat together in the bar. My hand reached across a rumpled quilt, the delicate trees and flowers of the blanket's pattern nearly invisible due to exposure to the sun.

"I don't want to go into it. There's a lot of baggage inside me right now. It's not your problem. It's mine. I'm a big girl, I knew what this would mean."

Her eyes deliberately avoided the used condoms I'd carelessly placed on the nightstand beside the bed. Their presence constituted a reminder that we were not meant to be, that our coming together was contrived.

"I need to get going."

"Can I see you before you leave?"

"I'm not sure."

"I can be in the restaurant at the Lodge by eight tomorrow morning," I suggested.

The ring of the telephone interrupted our reflective silence.

"Hello?" I whispered.

I glanced at the clock. It was nearly 1:00am.

"Mike, it's Beth."

"Beth. It's late. What's up?"

"You didn't call."

"Got tied up with the audit. I got back about ten thirty."

"I tried calling the hospital. They said you were done yesterday."

I was trapped. Roxanne sat quietly next to me. I understood the remorse depicted in her awkward glance. She was not wearing makeup. Her hair was wet. Her eyes seemed hesitant, as if ashamed to be listening to my conversation with my wife.

"There were some rough spots I needed to go over. I got a bite to eat and went back to the hospital to finish up. Everyone else had gone home by the time I got back." The lie was presented easily.

"I have some bad news," my wife revealed.

A lump formed in my throat.

"What?"

"Debra Jo died tonight."

My mind raced. I tried to recall an image of my best friend's daughter. Whether due to my fatigue or my infidelity, I couldn't retrieve a likeness of the little girl's face.

"How?"

"She had a cardiac arrest playing indoor soccer at the College."

"Goddamn it, you've got to be kidding."

"Mike, why would I tell you this if it wasn't true. Al needs you to call him. He was there. He tried to do CPR. There was nothing he could do. Her aorta ruptured. She was gone before the paramedics arrived."

I drew Roxanne's hand to mine. I didn't reflect upon the awkwardness of the gesture. It didn't register that our embrace was inappropriate. The Canadian woman's eyes followed the movement of my mouth as I spoke.

"I'll call him right away," I promised.

"He needs you, Mike. He's devastated, blames himself for pushing her into sports."

A portrait of Al, his body wracked and torn by grief as he tried to call the soul of his little girl back, as he tried to make a deal with God to save her, displaced all other images in my mind.

"I'll call him."

"When are you coming home?"

I glanced at Roxanne. Bare skin sloped provocatively from her collarbone and disappeared beneath the terrycloth fabric of the bath towel. I wanted to touch her, to follow the water's path across her skin with my fingers.

"As soon as I get done calling Al."

"It's a long ways. Drive carefully."

"I will."

A moment of utter, unbelievable quiet infiltrated the room. I hung up the receiver.

"What happened?" the woman asked.

I didn't answer.

"You're upset."

I envisioned a pretty little girl running across the artificial surface of the School of Mines Fieldhouse. My face contorted as I watched, in horrific detail, the child grimace and fall to the floor, her joy dispelled by cruel genetics and fate.

"Mike, what's wrong?"

"My friend Al."

I left the thought unfinished.

"The State Trooper?"

I nodded.

"Something happened to his daughter," I said, my voice bearing an inflection of harshness.

I recognized that the woman I was with was someone special. That she would remember details about my friend's life, a person she'd never met, struck a chord deep within me.

"She died playing soccer," I whispered in a softer tone. "Her heart gave out."

"Oh God, no. Wasn't she like six years old?"

"Seven."

The woman's eyes filled with tears. She turned towards me. I held Roxanne as tightly as I could, knowing full well that nothing more would ever happen between us.

SHORT STORIES

FRESH AIR

I'm not sure why it happened. I know it was my fault. There's no doubt about it. Jared told me so before he left me. Try as I want to, I can't change what took place. The past is what it is and no amount of wishful thinking can alter history. I hoped things would be different. Then I wouldn't be alone, then I wouldn't be in the place that I'm in.

Years of regret flood over me at night, when I'm by myself, when the sun has disappeared, cloaking me in evening's shame. The thing is, I've become certain that death is the only way I can ease my burden. Statistically that should happen in about thirty years. I don't know if I can make it that long.

Jared was tall and muscular, blond with blue eyes, the captain of our high school football team and the son of a Lutheran minister. Some folks said I was pretty as a young girl. Everyone said I was beautiful as a young woman. I don't know about that. When I met Jared Wilson, I recall quite clearly that I had skinny legs, dark, forlorn eyes, and that I stuffed my Playtex bra with tissue paper in a desperate attempt to create cleavage.

I didn't like the way my face, with its stark cheekbones and unyielding angles, carried shadows. I recall spending hours trying to insure my make-up was just right so that the clean edges of my harsh profile became soft and feminine. I remember sitting in front of a mirror, slowly drawing bright red lipstick across my thin lips, all the while wishing I had a full, luscious mouth like Natalie Wood. Thinking about what happened later on, it's odd, almost spooky, how much I idolized her.

Jared and I met at Proctor High School, Proctor, Minnesota being a small railroad town located on the outskirts of Duluth. By the time we entered tenth grade, Bob Dylan had already left his birthplace for the bright lights of more sophisticated venues. I suspect Dylan left

Northeastern Minnesota because there were no artists, no musicians, no beat poets around here in the late 1960's. Back then, Duluth harbored blue-collar workers, lots of smoke, ships, railroads, and iron ore, but few artisans. Unlike Bobby Zimmerman, I never left.

Like I said, people claimed I was beautiful. After high school, Jared went off to Gustavus Adolphus College in St. Peter, Minnesota. I stayed home, attending the nursing program at The Villa, the College of St. Scholastica, a local Catholic girl's school. My senior year in college, the year I was voted "Miss Duluth", I also became pregnant.

"How the hell did this happen?" Jared lamented as we sat in the front seat of his '48 Ford Coupe on Skyline Boulevard overlooking Duluth.

It was October of 1970. Vietnam was all over the news. Some of my friends saw their lovers off to fight. I was lucky. Jared had a scholarship and a deferment. We spent a lot of time together that summer. Sometimes we parked on the boulevard and petted ourselves into a hormonal frenzy. I resisted going any further, in yielding my virginity, for as long as I could. From what I've told you, it's obvious that Jared's primal urges proved to be overwhelming.

"Just bad luck," I said.

I avoided eye contact with him as we spoke. A moonless evening cast its pallid cloth over us, creating an atmosphere appropriate for the discussion. The yellow, red, and white lights of the city shimmered below. Out of the corner of my eye I watched Jared's grip tighten on the hard plastic of the car's steering wheel. Green light, illumination from the Ford's instrument panel, artificially brightened my lover's face. Fearing what I'd find in his eyes, I fixed my gaze on the cracked vinyl surface of the dashboard.

"Luck? What's luck got to do with it?" Jared muttered. "We only did it twice. How the hell did you end up pregnant? I thought you told me you were safe?"

"I thought I was. Look, it only takes one sperm out of millions to make a baby," I lectured. "You could've used protection, you know."

"I would have if you would have been square with me."

"What the hell is that supposed to mean?"

I wanted to lash out and strike him in the face.

In reality, we had intercourse three times that I could remember, if you discount the eight or nine times Jared ejaculated in my hand. To make matters worse, as I recall it, I never attained orgasm before becoming pregnant. That night, I thought of using Jared's sexual ineptitude against him. I didn't.

"It's just that a baby screws the whole thing up."

I waited a minute, allowing the warmth of the Ford's heater to float over my shivering body as I thought about options. But in 1970, in Duluth, Minnesota, there were few options available for girls who had the bad luck to turn up pregnant.

Sure, there were rumors of abortions. There were stories that this one or that one had been to see an unlicensed surgeon in some filthy duplex on some shady street. But I didn't know those women. I didn't want to contemplate the sin of killing my child, of watching its lifeblood dragged from my womb. Severing the maternal connection to my fetus, whether by abortion or adoption, seemed implausible.

"Do you love me?" I asked.

There was an elaborate pause. Jared removed his hands from the steering wheel and dug his fingers into the corduroy fabric of his slacks. I knew his response would be a lie. I didn't care.

"Yes."

"Then we might as well get married," I urged, ignoring his deception. "If we get it done fairly soon, I won't be showing."

It was my turn to lie. My abdomen was already distended, making it increasingly uncomfortable for me to wear slacks.

"I didn't want it to be like this. I wanted to do it on my own terms," Jared whined.

"I think it's a little late for that now," I advised.

He quit college. A little Irish priest, someone my parents knew, Father Daniel O'Halloran, married us in St. Rose Catholic Church in Proctor. It was a private ceremony with just family and a few close friends. I finished school and graduated before the baby came. Jared took a job in Duluth working as a policeman.

Diana's birth wasn't easy. My labor with her was four hours of concentrated pushing, of urging my loins and buttocks to move the reluctant baby through the birth canal. When the top of her head emerged, tearing my delicate femininity as easily as a knife passes through cotton, I couldn't reach out to Jared for solace or support.

Back in 1971, Duluth hospitals didn't allow fathers to be present in the delivery room. As I grunted and strained to bring our daughter into the world, I struggled alone. In brief moments of lucidity, I imagined my husband, his large hand impatiently pushing clean wisps of blond hair away from his forehead as he fretted.

After the baby, things got better between us. Jared learned patience, learned to listen to what I wanted from him as a husband, as a lover. I'm not sure that what we had was ever really love but I am certain it was a form of mutual respect and admiration.

When we bought our house on Moogie's Lake, a small pond of shallow, fetid water on the town border between Proctor and Hermantown, I felt like we were meant to be a family. I began to dream of another child, of bringing another life into our home.

Even though I no longer hold such a vision for myself, the house on the hill overlooking the north shore of the lake occupies a prominence in my memory.

Specters from the past rustle decaying cattails and marsh grass along what was once our lawn. The surface of the pond freezes, allowing thick ice to choke out any life unable to submerge itself in the lake's muddy bottom. I am troubled by nightmares. They are always the same.

In these dreams, my bare hands and face are cold. I think I know how to swim but it seems that I've forgotten that skill. My body, much smaller and lighter than I remember it, keeps falling, drifting deeper into the water, towards the foundation of Moogie's Lake. My hair, the strands tightly wound and freshly warm from a curling iron, trail behind me in the dank water. My mind plays tricks on me. My dolls and toys descend towards the lake bottom with me, as if someone has deliberately dumped them into the water.

Thick tendrils of underwater plants wrap themselves around the saturated wool of my pajamas and hold me fast. Small bubbles escape my mouth and float upward. The bubbles burst as they reach the surface, allowing carbon dioxide to mix with December air. Small ripples of pond water wash the fragile edges of the ice where I fell in. Though I am far beneath the waves, my ears hear the muted sound of a dog barking. The animal's voice seems distinctly urgent.

Feelings of panic are replaced by a sense of acceptance. I theorize that this is because my brain craves oxygen. As my fabric-covered feet settle into the black sludge of the lakebed, my lungs hesitantly fill with fluid. I can no longer see the light of day above me. I can no longer recall the faces of my parents. I can no longer resist the power of the lake.

The Monday it happened was a brutally cold December morning. I was smoking my fourth Lucky Strike of the day. I started smoking when I was pregnant. I started smoking because I needed the nicotine to get me through college graduation, through

61

our wedding, through the terror of childbirth. I never stopped.

The last of the *Today Show* weather forecast scrolled down the black and white screen of our Admiral portable television set. The TV rested solidly on the Formica surface of our kitchen countertop. Yellow and white linoleum flowed across the kitchen floor. The walls were painted a complimentary hue. Dark brown Gibson appliances, a built-in range and a small icebox, gave the room its only accent of color.

Drawing hard on a Lucky, I watched absently as a thin wisp of smoke rose over the sink where dirty Melmac cups and plates floated in soapy ooze. There was plenty of time left in the day for housework.

Raven's incessant barking drew my attention. I rose, escaping the grip of the soft vinyl seat of my kitchen chair. I caught a glimpse of myself in the oven window and admired my figure. The weight I'd gained with Diana was gone. I pressed my stomach inward with my free hand, cigarette held imperiously in the other, and considered whether or not I was still beautiful.

Secretive eyes stared back at me. My hair, freshly washed, pulled tight into a ponytail, shone with the exuberance of anticipated pregnancy. It had been four years since Diana's birth. It was time for another child, regardless of the toll on my body. I patted the soft fabric of my skirt, shifting the folds so that the tiny bluebell pattern of the cloth danced towards my ankles, and I smiled at the woman I left behind in the reflection.

The soft fibers of our living room carpeting, its color off-white, its texture, luxurious, cushioned my bare feet as I entered the room. My daughter's toys, her dolls, doll furniture, plastic dishes, and wooden blocks littered the area. I stopped to consider her teddy bear. The toy's head rested softly against a plastic cup as if the bear was sipping imaginary tea.

A faint orange haze, the remains of the early morning sun, meekly touched the fabric of the stuffed animal. During this unplanned interlude, I considered how amazing it was that I'd come to a place of contentment with both motherhood and marriage.

I looked out the window and surveyed the clean white snow covering our back yard. At the end of the incline of the lawn, Raven pranced feverishly along the shore of the lake, barking like a fool.

A cool breeze touched my face. My cigarette flared. I noticed that the back door was open.

"Oh my God," I screamed.

I rushed onto the rear porch. Though light snow was falling, I discovered footprints leading down the slope towards the pond. A thin crust of new ice was forming where my daughter had fallen through the lake's deceptive surface. The cold of a thousand ice ages descended over me as I ran through the bizarre beauty of cruelly waltzing snowflakes. Raven bounded towards the water's edge in panicked loyalty, desperate to provide me with assistance, but, as in my dream, I am unable to save myself.

TRAGEDY AT VERMILLION FALLS

Bucky Nevin wasn't always in this kind of trouble. Short and thick through the torso and neck, Bucky stood a shade under five-foot-eight but weighed somewhere over two-fifty. You couldn't knock Bucky off his feet with a two by four.

He got himself in trouble by forgetting to read the map. Oh, he knew that somewhere up ahead of him on the Vermillion River there were impassable falls. The Vermillion Falls. But that didn't impress Bucky to the point where he needed to know exactly where on the river the cascade was located.

Rain pelted Nevin as he sat quietly, concealed by wild rice, in a boat pulled tight against the muddy shoreline of the river. Champ, his best friend Jamison Towers' Springer Spaniel, sat ahead of him on the front seat of the pram. The dog looked sleek and powerful sitting on all fours as its yellow eyes scanned the sky for mallards.

A small flock of red-headed mergansers blew down the river channel oblivious to the string of seven mallard decoys, five hens and two drakes, that bobbed in the current in front of Nevin's hiding place. Bucky raised his Stevens automatic to his shoulder and followed the ducks with the muzzle of the weapon past the spit of sand, rushes, and rock he was anchored against. He did not fire. He did not want to have to clean and cook nasty fish ducks when the weather promised flights of giant greenheads winging in from Manitoba.

The dog whined as the mergansers raced off ahead of the impending storm.

"Calm down Champ. We're after mallards."

The hunter reached across the boat and stroked the wet fur of the dog with a gloved hand. Nevin was buttoned up against the elements. His camouflage raingear, insulated and snug around his wide body, kept him warm. His leather boots were laced tight. A silver steel lid to a thermos doubled as a coffee mug and rested precariously on the wooden seat next to him. Vapor rose from the cup, mingled with the moist air, and disappeared.

Jamison and another college kid, Kurt Whitney, were somewhere up-river, walking the far shore, hoping to jump ducks resting in the backwaters of the stream. Anything they missed would likely catch the breeze and pass by the point Bucky Nevin occupied. Nevin wasn't much of a shot; but then, given the element of surprise, he wouldn't need to be.

The hunter watched the wind buffet the birch and aspen trees lining the shorelines. He began to finger the trigger of the Stevens twenty gauge in anticipation of the kill. Nothing flew.

Crack. Crack. Crack.

The report of Jamison's Browning twelve echoed from deep within the weather. Nevin stared intently below the edge of the onrushing clouds in anticipation of a flight.

Twenty beautiful mallards, the leader large and emerald, came in furiously just above his hiding place. Bucky removed his right glove and brought a duck call to his lips. The plastic mouthpiece of the signal felt cold and brutal against his tongue.

"Quaaackk. Quaaackk..."

Nevin drew the call out in a forlorn invitation to his prey. The lead drake set its wings. The flock descended.

"Steady," Bucky Nevin counseled himself. "That's it. Come on in. That's it," he whispered. The reeds around him sang out with each gust of passing wind. Jamison's dog began to shiver with excitement.

"Stay...," Nevin murmured.

The hunter eased the walnut stock of the shotgun up to his right shoulder. He slid his hand along the steel undercarriage of the weapon until it was properly balanced. Slowly, nearly imperceptibly, he brought the receiver to his eye. The shift in his weight caused the gunwale of the pram to dip dangerously towards the water.

Crack. Crack. Crack.

The Stevens barked. Three small bursts of flame erupted from the barrel. Nevin's first shot was well behind the leader. His second was well below the entire flock. The pattern of the third round crumpled the second duck in the flight. The hen folded and splashed into the near-freezing water of the Vermillion River just beyond the edge of the weeds. The other mallards beat their wings in alarm and veered out of harm's way.

"Fetch," Bucky commanded, though Champ was already in mid-stride over the bow of the boat before Nevin spoke.

"Damn fine shot," the kid muttered to himself as he watched the dog paddle out into foam. Nevin took his eyes off the Springer to reload. When he looked up again, the dog was clearly in trouble.

Nevin hadn't realized that he was only two hundred yards from the rapids when he cut the Johnson outboard and drifted into shore to place his decoys. The hunter was oblivious to the fact that the full force of the river was gathered directly in front of him where the dog was struggling.

"I'll get you boy," the kid shouted over the roar of the stream and the storm. Nevin crawled to the bow of the pram and raised the anchor.

Thud.

Weeds, mud, and water dripped free of the iron weight as the hunter dropped the anchor into the boat. Nevin reached under a seat and removed a wooden oar; its oak shaft bleached gray by the elements. He pushed against the bottom of the river with the oar and moved the boat away from the shallows. Poling the vessel into the current's grip, Bucky watched the dog capture the drifting carcass in the middle of the swirling water.

"Good boy. Bring it here."

Champ worked feverishly against the river. The Spaniel didn't move. His efforts merely allowed him to remain suspended in place. Nevin floated the boat next to the churning dog, grabbed the Springer by the collar, and with one hand, hoisted fifty pounds of soaking wet dog and mallard to safety.

"That's a 'boy. Let's get the hell out'a here," the hunter said, pivoting on his rump to face the ten-horse. Bucky's bare fingers gripped the hard rubber handle attached to the motor's starter rope. Nevin drew the chord back with all his strength.

"Shit."

The hunter held a limp rope in his hand. The rope was no longer attached to the flywheel of the Johnson outboard motor. The pram began to bob and spin in the boiling water, captive of the stream's authority.

A wave of panic surged through Nevin's mind. Whether the dog sensed the man's fear or not, overwhelming dread descended upon the human. Bucky reached for the oars. Frantic, he tried to place the metal pins of the oars into the oarlocks. Precious time sped by as his bared fingers fumbled in the cold. Rocks, surrounded by dancing plumes of water, rose from the depths to complicate the boat's course. The hunter pulled with all his strength and weight against the oars. His effort slowed the forward progress of the craft but was no match for the terrible determination of the river.

Another squall rolled in. Thick rain pounded the painted metal skin of the boat. The square bow of the pram began to take on water. Nevin pulled hard to the left, then to the right, seeking to avert a head-on collision with a boulder. The boat slid sideways and became trapped against the immovable stone. Buck's eyes scouted the riverbed. Ahead, no more than thirty yards distant, the river disappeared completely from view. Noise from the waterfall blocked out the sound of the wind, the cry of the storm.

Nevin glanced upstream. A large spruce limb bounced to the current. The speed of the river's passing caused the dead tree to waltz in time to the Vermillion's pulse.

"Let's go," Bucky yelled. The dog wouldn't budge. Nevin tried to grab the animal's collar. The boat shifted, causing the right gunwale to dip beneath the surface. Nevin's life preserver floated away on the tongue of the river. Realizing that he had no other choice, the youth stood up and jumped towards the submerged spruce.

Water tore at the hunter's arms as he fought to grasp the tree. Unforgiving cold disrupted his ability to think. His left foot touched a stone. Using the river bottom for leverage, he pushed against the powerful embrace of the water. Swinging his arms wildly, one hand touched smooth, wet wood. Instinctively, Nevin's fingers wrapped around the deadhead. He pulled himself closer, grabbed another branch with his free hand, and hung on.

Bucky's eyes followed the half-submerged boat as it floated down the channel. The pram bounced off rocks like a ball bearing in a pinball machine. The dog's front paws remained firmly planted against the bow of the boat as the craft drifted along. If the Springer Spaniel knew what was in store for him, where he was headed, he betrayed no obvious recognition of his fate.

The exhausted hunter watched as Jamison's canine, Jamison's outboard motor and boat, along with Nevin's shotgun and hunting box, vanished over the precipice. Bucky expected to hear a crash, some sort of noise denoting the destruction of the property. Instead, all he heard was the constant hum of water and the incessant assault of the storm.

The other hunters rescued Nevin before nightfall. They found the remains of the duck boat the next morning. They found the pram, crumpled in half like a piece of discarded tinfoil, resting on a gravel bar three miles below the foot of the Vermillion Falls. The boat was empty. Its contents had been lost to the river. The dog was never seen again.

WAITING FOR EMILY

Ted Foresman had not seen Emily Sullivan in eight, maybe nine years. They'd gone to Washington Junior High together. Then Emily's dad took a job far from the Great Lakes; far away from the gray and cold that enveloped their city in bleak, unforgiving weather.

She was his best friend back at a time when he needed friends more than he needed money or objects; back when pimples defined a kid's level of popularity and when athleticism meant everything; back when he was a nerd and she was the captain of the cheerleading squad. He never understood why she lowered herself to be seen with him. He was short, inept at sports. His hazel blue eyes were hidden behind massive black plastic eyeglass frames. He was bright, in a bookish sort of way. He wasn't popular. She was.

A pungent pother of cigarette smoke hung low over the table. He was alone as he almost always was. The plastic eyeglass frames were gone, replaced by wire rims. His dark hair hung clean and fresh across the base of his neck, a far cry from the crewcut he sported the last time he was with her. His body was lean and strong from working out. He was no longer a skinny puke of a kid. He was a young man on the verge of going places.

His small hands cupped the cold surface of a beer mug. Thin fog spread out across the smooth texture of the glass due to the heat of his fingers. Ted pulled the sweet, liberating brew to his mouth and drained the container in one swallow.

"I'll keep in touch," she had promised that July morning, eight years distant.

"Ya, sure," he had replied, doubt strong and offensive in his voice.

"Really Ted. I'll write whenever I can."

They sat on her front porch. She was wearing a white tank top and a blue denim skirt. Thin, delicate straps held the cloth off her chest. Her skin was crimson, the result of trying to tan too quickly beneath the Northeastern Minnesota sun. The front of the top clung tightly to her chest. A strapless bra discretely covered her. Small beads of sweat appeared under her square jaw, slid down her neck, and followed the natural curves of her body.

His eyes looked away before she caught him staring at her. She was a friend, not his girl. He had no right to look at her that way. He was fourteen and girl-less. It seemed he was always girl-less.

"You'll write once or twice. But you'll remember to call Bruce," he said.

"I don't know about that. Bruce has been an absolute poop to me these last few weeks," she replied, averting her eyes.

He wondered about that. Did she look away because she knew that she was nearly a woman and he was still mostly a little boy?

"All Bruce wants to do is grab, grab, grab. Or make out. Or drink. You're different," She said, returning her gaze towards him, her emotions revealed in a melancholy grin. A gesture of pity? A smirk of regret? He couldn't remember it that exactly.

"I'm a peach," he whispered under his breath, hoping that she wouldn't hear.

"Yes you are. You treat me like a person. Bruce Van Horn can't talk about books, or art, or music. That's why you and I will always be friends."

Friends. They'd known each other for two years. They met in Miss Beckwith's English class in eighth grade. Emily loved Hemingway. So did he, especially *Big Two-Hearted River*. A small brook trout stream flowed near the kid's house up in the hills, flowed down the steeps above the city until it disappeared in a culvert on its way to Lake Superior. He fished it every summer, nearly every day. He had the time. He didn't have a girl.

"Gotta go. The moving truck is leaving."

71

She stood up and carefully pressed her skirt flush against her sunburned legs with small, dainty hands. He looked at her face. She didn't wear make-up. She didn't need to. Emily's eyes were gray, large, and honest. Her lips were wide and red and concealed straight white teeth. She wasn't beautiful like her friends Sue and Joanne. She was simply real. Even at fourteen he knew that. He knew it because there were so few girls who were, or who ever are, real.

"Goodbye, Ted," she murmured as she kissed his cheek. A faint scent of perfume enticed his nostrils as she walked away. He watched her feminine sway carry her towards an old blue Bonneville. Her brother and sister were already in the back seat. He stood there, watching her duck into the car. He didn't say a word. He wanted to run after her, to tell her that Bruce was an asshole; that just because a guy can throw a football forty yards or sink free throws doesn't really matter. Instead, he watched helplessly as a cloud of blue exhaust erupted from the Pontiac's tailpipe. Then she was gone.

Teddy kept his part of the promise. So did she-to a point. They wrote to each other every month for the next few years. She made the cheerleading squad at her new high school. She fell in and out of love. He mostly tried to become someone, something that his body wouldn't let him be. He worked hard during the summers to become a football player. His father wanted it for him. It wasn't to be. He sat on the bench, never better than second or third string. Too small, too slow, too timid to play the game the way it was meant to be played.

Over time, their letters were reduced to strained attempts at politeness. There was no use in sending them but they did. His missives were filled with news about kids that she knew, kids she left behind in the city. Hers were mostly stories about her family, about people and places that Ted Forseman didn't care about.

During basic training, he actually wrote more often. He was bored. Not with the physical part of being at Paris Island. He relished the running, the mud, the exercise. He was bored with the Marine Corps mentality, the smallness of their thinking, their belief that war is inevitable and that men need to be ready to sacrifice themselves for honor. The hypocrisy made him smile inside. His time in basic training coincided with Nixon's resignation and the beginning of the end for South Vietnam. It forced recruits like Teddy to learn a new chain of command. Gerald Ford replaced Nixon at the top of the chain.

She didn't write much after he moved to a base on the West Coast. He knew he'd crossed some invisible line by writing to her during basic training from a base only a few hours away from her home. Or perhaps it was his phone call that had unnerved her.

"Emily Sullivan?"

"Yes."

"Don't you know who this is?" he'd asked, not realizing that, when they last talked, his voice was a full octave higher.

"I'm sorry. Do I know you?"

"It's Teddy, Teddy Foresman."

There had been a long pause.

"My God it's been years. It didn't recognize your voice, Ted. How are you?"

Though her words seemed sincere, Ted sensed a hint of uneasiness during their conversation.

"Is anything wrong? You don't sound too happy to hear from me," he interjected.

"No, nothing like that. You just took me by surprise is all."

The rest of the five minute telephone call wasn't much better. They said little of substance and made vague, half-hearted promises to remain in touch. He never wrote to her again. He was finished with the fantasy, finished with the dream, until she called him.

"Teddy."

It was a Saturday a year after his honorable discharge from the Marines. His mom, her hair still up in curlers, her mascara stained by tears from another all-night argument with Ted's father, shook him by the shoulders as he curled deep inside his bedcovers.

"Damn it Ted, wake up. There's some girl on the phone for you."

His eyes fought against the memory of the eighteen or nineteen brandy Cokes he'd ingested the night before. His hair was slick with sweat as he pushed the unruly strands away from his eyes. He tried to focus on his mother's face. She looked as bad as he felt.

"What?" he answered weakly.

"There's a girl on the telephone. Says her name is Emily Sullivan. You know her?"

"Someone I used to know," he said quietly, "a long time ago."

"Long time ago? You're only twenty-three-years old. What the hell is a long time ago to you?"

Abbie Foresman turned away from her son, muttering to herself as she retreated from his bedroom. The young man strained to raise himself from his bed as he reached for the telephone.

"Em, is that you?" he asked, his tongue thick with liquor as he spoke.

"Yes, it's me. I'm in town for Spring Break. Sue, Joanne, and I are flying down to Florida tomorrow but I thought I'd try to see you, to make up for how shitty I was when you were at Paris Island."

"You weren't shitty. I didn't have any business calling you," he lied.

"Sure you did. You were always there to listen to me when I bitched. I never really knew why. But you were always there."

I was always there because I was in love with you, he thought. *Don't paint me with some saintly motive. I wanted to be with you. I still do.* Ted Foresman wanted to say the words out loud but didn't.

"Are you busy tonight?"

Her question stunned him.

"Nope. Nothing going. Why?"

"I'd like to see you. I'm gonna stop in and see Bruce at his dad's pharmacy. Then I'd like to go out and do the town with my oldest, best bud."

"Where do you want to meet?" he asked.

Ted's heart raced. Testosterone pumped through his body like hot water through a radiator.

"You pick. I haven't been in this town for a long, long time."

He tried to speculate what the girl he once knew would look like as a woman. Her eyes would be the same. Her breasts, the squareness of her jaw, the whiteness of her skin, all the same. Her voice was different. He knew that from the phone call. There was a trace of the South in her diction, in her words, revealing sensuality and adulthood foreign to his knowledge of the girl that had left town so long ago.

"O'Gara's over in Superior is nice. What time should we meet?"

"I'll be there by seven," she said through a nervous laugh. "I can't wait."

He sat at a round Formica table. The tavern had no windows. His watch told him that it was half past seven. Outside, it was night. Wind whipped across the decaying ice of Lake Superior. He contemplated where he was, where his life was headed, as he often did when he drank alone. He was smart enough to know that his drinking was getting out of hand. The boozing wasn't hurting his grades at the local college where he was enrolled in a law enforcement program. The alcohol wasn't affecting his part-time job as a security guard. But the residual effect of drinking hard four to five times a week was undeniably taking a toll. It was harder than ever for him to get up for his three mile run in the morning. It was harder to shake off the lingering impact of the hangovers and concentrate in class.

It might have been different if he had a steady girlfriend. As far as he could tell, there weren't any women interested in him at school. All the tan, tight college coeds ogled the jocks. All the unattractive ones wanted anyone they could latch onto and turn into a husband. Maybe Emily Sullivan would be different. Maybe something deep inside her compelled her to seek him out. Maybe.

"Can I get another Schlitz?" he asked.

The waitress, far too old to be of interest to him or in him, nodded. Teddy's eyes followed the woman as she did her job. Her gestures were full of exhaustion. Every movement was a chore, an ordeal. He wondered what kind of life one would have to live to be so defeated.

Is this my third or fourth beer? he asked himself as the tired woman slid another glass of honey-colored draft across the tabletop.

She retrieved a soggy dollar bill; the paper wet from spilled beer, from the table's plastic surface, and pushed sixty-five cents towards Teddy. He shoved the coins back at the woman.

"Keep the change."

He didn't normally tip. Tonight, with Emily Sullivan on the way, he felt generous. The waitress claimed the money and moved on. If she appreciated the gesture, she didn't show it.

Wild, primitive thoughts, visions of making love to Emily preoccupied Ted Forseman's mind. He smiled as he thought of her soft hair touching his face, its sheen dancing in the light of a dozen candles. Muted conversation from other patrons in the joint did not disturb his revelry. He was no longer fourteen; no longer afraid to tell her what he felt when he looked into her eyes. He closed his eyes and tried to recall the pattern of her lips touching his cheek as she kissed him goodbye.

It was getting late. He broke his vow to remain sober. He ordered another Schlitz with a shot of Everclear on the side. Somewhere behind the bar a telephone rang.

"Is Ted Foresman here?" a male bartender asked.

The barkeep was a short, burly man with thick black hair covering his arms. He held a plastic telephone receiver over his head as he addressed the crowd. Thirty to forty men and women engaged in deep, important conversation ignored the man's inquiry. Foresman tilted his head and slammed down the last of the grain alcohol. The Everclear seared his throat on its way to his liver. The floor seemed to move beneath Ted as he rose from his chair and walked towards the bar. His thinking was clouded, his outlook sullen, as he picked up the telephone receiver.

"Teddy, is that you?" a female voice asked.

He didn't answer. What was there to say?

"I'm really sorry. I don't think I'm going to be able to make it over there tonight," the woman explained.

Her words were shallow. Even in his drunken stupor, Teddy Foresman knew that she was with someone else. A better offer, likely Bruce's offer, had won out.

"Ted are you there?"

Emily's voice, though colored by the exotic inflection of Dixie, no longer interested him. Teddy Foresman steadied himself with one hand on an adjacent barstool. The booze had numbed him but he wasn't about to be deceived. He knew that he and Emily Sullivan had never been; that they would never be. There was no reason to belittle his ego further by responding to the woman. He placed the telephone receiver on top of the bar and walked out the door.

THE BEGINNING ROOM

Allison Korinen followed her stepfather, Robert McCray across the barnyard. The McCray farm occupied sixty acres of poor rocky land in Northeastern Minnesota. Robert drank better than he farmed. He was drunk as he pulled the girl into a dark shed and shut the door behind them.

"Know why you're here?" Robert asked her, his tongue thick with brandy.

"No," she answered.

Allie was lying. Megan, her older sister, had told Allie about the room. Robert used his body to keep Allison away from the door. She was trapped by his lust. In the poor light, the man's ugly, pockmarked face stared at her. A smell of booze and sweat permeated the thick air. Though she could not see the details of Robert's clothes, she knew that they were filthy.

"This is where it begins."

His hand touched her freshly washed blond hair as he spoke. His fingers vacated her hair and stroked the softness of her cheek. The pungent smell of cows on his skin made her turn away. Robert grabbed her by the throat and forced her to look into his eyes, eyes that bore no resemblance to anything human.

"Don't look away," he said in an angry tone. "I taught Megan. Now I'm gonna' teach you."

McCray's hand found the buttons of the girl's shirt. A scream built up inside Allison and rushed to escape her throat. The man fumbled with the fasteners. A thick palm pressed against her mouth, forcing her to taste the bovine urine impregnated in his flesh. Her eyes bulged with horror. A hand slid underneath the garment.

"You're not wearing a bra," the farmer observed. "You best do so from now on. You need to be covered up lest the boys 'round here start getting fancy ideas."

She let out a muffled cry as his fingers touched the skin above her sternum. He forced her body deeper into the room, pressing her away from the door, away from her mother.

When McCray was finished, their bodies remained locked together, cushioned by oat straw. He kissed her full on the lips with sour breath.

"If you tell your mother, I'll deny it," he whispered. "Your momma won't take your word against mine. Best thing for all concerned is for you to keep your mouth shut."

Robert sat up and stroked the girl's hair. She didn't feel his touch. She was numb. She wondered if she would ever be capable of feeling anything again.

"Besides, you're just as guilty of sin as me," he added defensively.

The dairy farmer stared hard at her. His expression told her that he approved of her silence.

"That's it. Keep it to yourself. This here'll be our place, Allie, yours and mine."

After that, Robert McCray brought Allison to the shed once a week. One day, during seventh grade English, Allie felt sick. Slow, sticky warmth spread between her legs and forced her to run to the girl's lavatory. She sat in a stall hemorrhaging into the toilet until her mother came. Allison's first menstrual period proved to be a blessing. Fertility forced Robert to stop taking her to the Beginning Room.

"Where's Missy?" Margaret McCray asked Allison and Megan, her two oldest daughters, as the three of them worked in the kitchen a few weeks after Allison's incident at school. Missy was ten. She was the youngest of the Korinen girls. Mrs. McCray continued to knead a thick square of bread dough with her hands as she spoke.

"I saw her with Robert just a minute ago," Megan volunteered, her own hands deep in flour and eggs.

Generally, Margaret's face revealed profound sadness. Allison glanced at her mother's eyes. Something other than sadness was forming beneath her mother's expression.

"See if you can find Missy," her mother directed.

Without rinsing their hands, the sisters went outside. A bitter northwest wind stung their exposed skin. Allison spoke as they walked towards the barn.

"Meg, we can't..."

The older sister cut Allison short:

"I know. She's just a baby. We can't let it happen to her."

Though the door to the shed was closed, familiar sounds greeted the girls from within.

"Wait here," Megan commanded, her voice low and serious.

Allie pressed her body against the wall of the shed. Megan disappeared into the adjacent barn. Seconds later, she reappeared carrying an iron pry bar.

"What are you doing?" Allison gasped.

"I'm gonna' put an end to it," Megan replied tersely.

"No you're not," an adult voice interjected.

The girls' mother emerged from the shadows as she spoke.

"I'll deal with Robert," Margaret said, removing the metal tool from her oldest daughter's grip.

The sounds from within the shed stopped. Mrs. McCray opened the door. The weather concealed the creaking of the hinges. Nothing concealed the sound of solid iron striking the base of Robert McCray's skull.

Margaret exited the shelter with her youngest child in her arms. Missy fussed with a set of greasy handprints staining the front of her sweater as her mother carried her away from the building.

"Did he...?" Megan asked hesitantly.

"No. I was in time. I should've done it a long time ago," the mother replied as she handed the heavy iron bar to Allison.

"Wash this off and put it in the garage. Megan, you take Missy on up to the house and put her to bed."

Mrs. McCray strode defiantly into the shed. Kneeling beside her husband, she gauged the labored rise and fall of his chest. Blood was pooling on the hard concrete floor beneath the man's head. The woman dug into her husband's shirt pocket and found a pack of Camel Straights. Lighting a cigarette, she drew heavily against the burning tobacco. Her effort caused the ember to flare.

Studying the man's face by the light of the cigarette, the woman exhaled vigorously, sending a cloud of smoke into the stale air of the shed. She placed the Camel in Robert's limp hand, feeling no remorse as hot ash fell onto brittle straw. Flames sputtered, igniting the dry fodder. The fire began to lap at the edges of the slumbering man's clothing. Flames blackened Robert's skin as his wife stood up and walked out of the building.

Outside, Margaret watched tongues of flame engulf the Beginning Room. Fueled by dry lumber and a quickening wind, the blaze engaged the entirety of the shed and the attached barn. Robert McCray's funeral pyre illuminated the yard.

"Accidents happen," Margaret said softly beneath her breath, a glimmer of hope forming within her pale blue eyes.

ON THE ROAD

There was quiet in the house as the woman, looking vulnerable and alone, began to sing. Her voice was thin and soft, like a blade of pasture grass before the summer sun hardens it:

Now that the song is over
Now that the chords are done
Will you put your head down
Please rest inside my song.

and sleep my darling child
for the night is over
just shut your tired eyes
the long day is over.

Now that the tunes have ended
Now that the notes have left
Close your eyes and
Calm your worried breath

and sleep my darling child
the long night is over
please calm your fainting heart
the long day is over.

What would you do if the stars never shone
Would you leave me here by myself?
What would you say if the crowd didn't smile
Would you empty your pockets and go?

Now that the song is over
Now that the birds will rise
Will you rest here and
Close your tired eyes

and sleep my loving child

for the night is over
please lay your body down
see how quick it's over.

There was a moment, as the last chord of the song, a hauntingly beautiful ballad, drifted across the thick air of the crowded coffeehouse, of inexplicable anticipation. As the folksinger's hands came to rest in her lap, an old Harmony six-string guitar hanging loose from its strap, the woman lowered her head in reverence to her muse.

"All right," someone in the crowd yelled. The outburst drew a symphony of applause as those in attendance stood in tribute.

"Encore," another voice cried out.

The singer appeared spent. She'd already played two encores for her admiring fans. Amy Maddox had no more to give: no more words, no more songs, no more music.

"Thanks for coming. I hope to see you all tomorrow night," she replied in the rehearsed voice that her adoring public had come to expect.

The lights came up. Maddox disappeared behind the cheap canvas wall dividing stage from dressing room.

"Great show, Amy," an old man, his head crowned with a "Cook County Vikings" baseball cap said to the musician as he handed her a can of cold Pepsi.

The singer's hands were rough and callused, the result of playing gigs on the road nearly every day of the year.

Two hundred and five shows this past year alone, she thought as she studied the damaged skin holding the soda.

The shows all blurred together in her mind. They formed one event, one singular concert in her brain. No individual performance stood out from any other.

"Thanks. Some of it went pretty well, though that last encore really sucked."

"Your fans sure didn't think so. They loved it. You could've heard a pin drop in the place."

A bead of crystalline sweat rolled down the woman's right temple. She brushed the moisture away with the back of her hand and drank deeply of the soft drink before sitting heavily in an over-stuffed armchair. The chair's covering was faded from use. If Amy Maddox had looked at the cloth with any degree of scrutiny, she would've noted a diminished pattern to the fabric. Forget-me-nots formed an intricate, ghostly design across the furniture, the details of which had been reduced to mere impressions by years of hard use.

"Max van Zeldt. You're such a sweetheart. Maybe after a couple of more shows your lies will turn into the truth," she offered in response.

Van Zeldt's Coffeehouse in Grand Marais was a venue that folk artists traveling through the Upper Midwest dreamed of playing. The venue was located at the tip of the Arrowhead Region of Northeastern Minnesota, on the shores of Lake Superior only a half-hour's drive from the Canadian Border. Though it was a tortuous two-hour drive from the outskirts of Duluth to the diminutive village, the presence of Max Van Zeldt, former record producer and personal friend of John Prine, made a show at Van Zeldt's place an essential part of any folk singer's tour of the state.

The Coffeehouse was located in an old variety store along the west side of Grand Marais' main street. Plate glass display windows overlooked a marina and the bay. In the summer, tourists from the Twin Cities sipped cappuccino and espresso while watching the angular movements of elegant sailboats headed towards the deep water of the lake. Maddox was performing in the winter. The windows were obstructed by insulated drapes in a feeble attempt to keep the place warm.

"That's a pile of crap and you know it. *The Song is Over* is one of my favorites. Tonight's version was as good as it gets."

The singer pulled a pack of Marlboro Lights out of her purse and struck a match. She leaned into the flame and drew heavily on the cigarette. Her skin, tan and healthy, defied her two-pack-a-day habit and glistened under the subtle backstage lighting. Amy kicked off her unlaced Converse All Stars, the bare skin of her feet as tan and youthful looking as the color of her cheeks. Small laugh lines accented her smile. Her mouth, pouty and expressive, blew rings of ghostly smoke into the upper reaches of the space. She was deliberate and agile in her movements, not at all like the self-conscious stage persona she afforded her fans.

Max had tried to score with her the first time she played Grand Marais. Amy politely told the promoter to "fuck off". The rejection hadn't seemed nearly so harsh coming from her. The petite woman's light brown eyes, her tiny body, and long blond hair had immediately taken in the club owner. It was obvious to Van Zeldt that Amy Maddox's hair color was artificial. Hints of gray, a betrayal of her age, thirty-three, were the give away. This minor deception didn't matter. The Dutchman knew what he wanted. Hair coloring wasn't high on his list of things to be concerned about.

He tried not to stare as she bent over, as Amy slid her tennis shoes under the chair and pulled nearly new leather hiking boots onto her bare feet. It was impossible for the old man not to follow the hesitant bounce of her breasts beneath the thin fabric of her cotton turtleneck.

"Thanks for the Pepsi. I think I'll head over to the café and get a bowl of soup before I turn in. See you tomorrow."

She stood up and gave the old man a discrete peck on the cheek.

"Like I said, hell of a show tonight," Max replied, hopeful that the singer hadn't detected his indiscretion.

"Flattery won't change my answer. It's still 'no'".

Amy worked her way into a heavy wool coat; the navy blue cloth cut so that it covered her narrow hips.

She pulled a black woolen watch hat down over her ears and covered her fingers with tattered blue mittens. The singer wore no jewelry. All the same, to Max Van Zeldt, Amy Maddox remained one of the most striking women he'd ever come across.

"You can't blame an old letch for trying."

"Sure I can. Don't you watch the public service ads? 'No' means 'no', Max. What part of that is so tough for you to understand?" she scolded teasingly.

As the woman opened the door she reached back and touched the promoter's face with a fabric-covered index finger.

"Maybe if we were only a decade apart, I'd feel differently. But you're like, what, seventy? That's too big a gap to make it work."

"Seventy-three. But a youthful seventy-three," Van Zeldt chirped.

An appreciative snicker escaped from the singer as she headed out into the February night.

The soup was good; bluefin herring, freshly netted from Lake Superior by the last remaining Norwegian fishing family in Cook County, was boiled with potatoes, corn, and cream into chowder. She ate quickly, downing a big tumbler of whole milk and three slices of stone-ground wheat bread with real butter along with the soup.

Walking the three blocks back up the hill to her rental cabin, along the road that eventually becomes the Gunflint Trail, she studied the deep void of the sky and tried to count the stars. It was no use. There were too many. She lost track of the number of universes revealed to her. The northern sky disclosed a plethora of distant worlds; precious stones hoarded by God.

"God, the omnipresent intergalactic miser," she mused.

Amy Maddox had been born in California, in Torrance, right next to LA. There were no stars, despite the heavenly origin of the name of the largest city in California, revealed to her during her childhood. It was only after she became a college student in Duluth and took a physical education course that included a canoe trip into the Boundary Waters Canoe Area, a wilderness dotted with lakes, streams and millions of acres of swamp and forest along the Minnesota-Ontario border, that she became aware that stars could actually be seen from earth with clarity once you escaped the smog and lights of LA.

Her rental unit was cold. The woman caretaker had turned down the electric baseboard heater again. Amy Maddox longed for a hot shower but knew that she needed to warm up the room before stripping down to her bare skin. Her gloved hand found the light switch and the thermostat, an old Honeywell device installed sometime after World War II. The singer turned up the heat. Meager warmth began to seep into the drab confines of the cabin. Amy kept her boots on. She activated the television, an out-dated color console, by using the set's ponderous remote control before collapsing on a battered davenport to await the arrival of heat.

Water cascaded across her skin. Turning her back to the glass door of the shower stall, the hot stream splashed off her buttocks. Amy became aware of an expectation of pleasure as she reached across the compartment and grabbed a bar of Dawn from the built-in chrome soap dish. Beads of water slipped past her closed eyes as she slowly curled and uncurled the feathery wisp of her pubic hair; hair that retained its natural color, a hue close in tone to the coat of a new-born fawn. The fibers were shaved smooth so that only the edges of her intimacy remained concealed. As she lathered the most private reaches of her body a wave of guilt assailed her and sought to deny her a moment of respite.

Thoughts of an unsuccessful tryst with someone she knew in Duluth, a married man, lingered. She fought against memory, working the soap and the suds, her hands far more patient and understanding than any male she'd ever been with. Under Amy Maddox's deft touch, her breathing became more rapid and external and the unpleasant images of that coupling retreated into the past.

Her pulse quickened. Intrigued by the familiarity of her own hand, she washed deeply. Finally, her chest heaving, her body assailed by passion, she sought the terrible finality of orgasm. But there was no climax, no resolution of the complex inner needs that defined her sexuality.

The brutal disappointment of another failed attempt at satisfaction arose within her. She slid down the smooth fiberglass wall of the shower stall. Sitting in the lotus position, the singer allowed water to assault her nakedness. Little pauses and gasps interrupted the flow of her tears as she tried to understand the nature of the burden weighing upon her soul.

"Am I always going to be this way?" she asked aloud.

After a time, she stood up. Seeking solace in routine, the folksinger emptied the contents of a Johnson's Baby Shampoo bottle onto the palm of her hand. The plastic container slid from her grasp and landed with a dull "thud" on the floor of the shower. Extending her hands above her head, she massaged the soap into her scalp as she tried to determine where it had all gone wrong.

Amy Maddox hadn't always lived without pleasure. There had been a time, years before, when most nights spent with a partner were, if not perfect bliss, at least in some sense of the word, fulfilling. Many of those occasions involved her abusing alcohol or pot to loosen up. There was something inside her, some germ of neurosis that demanded chemical assistance for her to achieve climax.

It was puzzling to her. She was gregarious and open, not at all ill at ease with men. The singer hadn't been abused, raped or, so far as she was aware, traumatized by sex at any time in her life so that any number of the therapists she'd seen could say:

"Ah yes, that's the reason..."

Certainly she'd experienced, in the quiet interludes after lovemaking, paradoxical moments of fleeting remorse. Though she'd been raised Mormon and no longer practiced the faith, she found that the years of religion were not so easily discarded. The spiritual consequences of casual sex routinely surfaced. But those were normal, ordinary feelings of human regret and were not, in her estimation, the cause of her dysfunction.

No one, least of all Amy Maddox herself, had been able to determine why, once she became sober, Amy's ability to make love became perfunctory and shallow.

The singer experienced no dreams of wonderful union, no fantasy worlds of unbridled passion as she slept in the single bed of the cabin. Denied the cavernous depths of post-coital slumber, the woman tossed and turned throughout the entirety of the night.

At daybreak, as the yellow globe of the sun crept above the thick winter ice of the lake, as the wind carried tiny bits of yesterday's snow across the open yard of the motel complex, the flakes glistening like incalculable miniature stars, the woman arose with no greater understanding of herself than when she first closed her eyes.

Breakfast at Margaret's Café on Saturday mornings is always crowded. Clean and bright eyed, at least on the exterior, the folksinger pulled on a faded pair of brown corduroys, the fabric close in tone to the natural color of her hair, over men's underwear. Over time, she'd come to appreciate the warmth and texture of flannel against her bare skin, and except for the times of the month that dictated against it, she wore men's boxers.

Given her slight bust, there had never been any need, and there still wasn't at age thirty-three, for her to defy the forces of nature by wearing a bra. She'd worn one once, when she was twelve with the expectation of greater things to come. Greater things in the chest department never did come, though no man she'd ever slept with mentioned her lack of cleavage as being a serious flaw.

Amy selected a white T-shirt and a gray and red plaid shirt from the clothes hanging in the room's only closet. She watched the sun rise slowly across the bay as she pulled the undergarment over her torso. Buttoning the front of the work shirt, the wool scratched her bare arms and neck. She left the buttons of the cuffs and collar undone.

Margaret's Café was surprisingly quiet. Visiting downhill skiers bound for Lutsen Mountain a few miles south of town apparently remained asleep beneath thick quilts of liquored slumber. It was past six. The restaurant had just opened. Amy's mittens gripped the brass handle of the entrance door. She began to pull the weight of the panel towards her when an unfamiliar voice interrupted her solitude:

"Let me get that for you."

The singer turned reflexively. A tall broad-shouldered man appearing to be in his early twenties reached out and pulled heavily on the door handle.

"Thanks."

She tried not to stare at the stranger. Though her work required her to expose her innermost thoughts and feelings through her art, experience had taught her to be guarded around strangers, especially men. There was often only one thing on their minds. And she, since her acceptance of sobriety, had seemingly sacrificed the ability to satisfy such desires in return for the ability to live out her life.

Still, her eyes were drawn to his. There was nothing she could do to avoid staring at the stranger. Slight pools of blue, the color of the sky just beneath the horizon, looked back at her. His face was tanned; not as hers was from hours spent in repose under man-made light, but colored by time spent out in the elements. The contours of his face were accented by the presence of a thick, honey-colored beard. There were no gray hairs peeking out from the forest of blond. Thick corn-colored hair, the ends cropped short, hung below the knitted limits of a red stocking cap. The man held the door for Amy as the singer entered the Café.

"I really enjoyed your show last night."

Maddox stopped, uncertain of how to respond. Many times in her past she'd heard that same line used as an opening gambit, as the beginning stanza in a difficult tango. But the texture of his voice, his intent, seemed removed from any attempt at false flattery. She pondered, in the instant available to her as they stood waiting to be shown their respective tables, whether to reply. The young stranger looked away. His eyes scanned a menu posted on the wall behind the lunch counter.

"It wasn't one of my better nights," she murmured.

Amy spoke with conviction, having decided to test the man's character. If he responded rashly, with unfettered zeal for her performance, the discussion would politely end. If his reply contained an element of self-restraint, she might allow a dialogue.

"It can't be easy performing in front of strangers night after night. But I still think your songs carry a powerful message. Plus I really like the way you pick out the base notes and don't simply resort to pulling off tired old chords."

Amazing, she thought. *He understands the guitar. God, he's so damn young. What the hell am I doing?*

"Table or booth?"

A waitress interrupted their brief introduction to each other. The woman was in her mid-fifties, dressed in blue jeans and a sharply pressed denim shirt with the words "Margaret's Café" embroidered across the top of the left pocket.

"We're not together," the musician responded.

Amy watched the man's reaction out of the corner of one eye. The singer was curious to see how he would respond to her disclosure.

"Are you waiting for someone?" he asked gently.

There it was. An opening move. Maddox knew that hesitation on her part might spell the end of an intriguing morning.

God knows I can use some intelligent company, she thought.

Being on the road, other than perfunctory conversations with promoters and roadies, she really wasn't able to just sit and enjoy another human being's company.

Go for it, she told herself.

"Nope," she finally admitted.

"Mind if I join you?"

"That'd be fine."

"Smoking or non-smoking?" the waitress asked as she contemplated the patrons beginning to form behind the two love-struck customers.

"Non...," the man caught himself in mid-sentence.

"I'm sorry. Do you smoke?" he asked.

"Yes but it doesn't matter. If it bothers you, I don't need to."

"A little smoke won't kill me," the handsome stranger said to the impatient waitress.

"Smoking, please."

They followed the server to a booth set against a wall of frosted glass overlooking the jetty occupied by the Grand Marais lighthouse. He helped her take off her coat. With athletic ease, the tall man removed his Carhart jacket. Amy noted that the fabric of the garment was devoid of the customary oil stains associated with such apparel. Her new companion sat down across from her in the booth. Looking intently at the menu, the young man removed his stocking cap, shook his hair, and tucked the hat into the waistband of his jeans.

"I'm William," he disclosed, extending his right

hand. "William Martin."

The singer's fingers met those of her companion over the surface of the table. His handshake was firm; his fingers strong and well proportioned.

"Pleased to meet you William. I'm Amy, Amy Maddox," she replied nervously.

It dawned her as she spoke that the revelation of her name was unnecessary. He'd paid for a ticket, seen her perform. He already knew her name. In fact, if he'd truly listened to her songs, digested her lyrics, William Martin already knew a great deal more about Amy Maddox than she might ever know about him.

"Bill. Call me Bill."

"OK. So Bill, what do you do in this cold little place?"

"I work for the Forest Service, the Feds. I'm in forest management."

"What's that mean?"

"Well, I'm a botanist by training. I help manage the sale of timber to loggers and logging companies. I try to insure they don't cut down all the old growth trees."

An involuntary smile crept across the singer's face. She liked "Bill" from Grand Marais. There was no hint of trepidation, no display of uncertainty about him as they spoke. Amy felt comfortable listening to his Northern Minnesota accent. She'd been in the state long enough to lose most of the attributes of her Southern California upbringing, including the inflections of LA in her speech. Her own diction was slowly and most assuredly becoming colored by her life in Duluth.

"Where'd you go to college?" she asked.

"Bemidji State. It's got a great environmental program."

"I've played that campus a lot. Great location, right on the lake and everything. The kids there are easy to play for."

Bill looked intently at the woman. His gaze was steady and determined but not rude.

"Have you always lived here, in Minnesota, I mean?" she asked.

"I was born in Moorhead but I fell in love with this part of the state. I came over here for a Boy Scout Jamboree when I was twelve. How about you?"

Amy's mind was preoccupied with thoughts of failure in the bedroom. Here she was, talking to a handsome guy, a younger man, as if she could satisfy him, as if she could placate the needs and desires that all men like him harbor.

Why put myself in a position to be disappointed again? she wondered.

She'd always loved kids. There was a time, seven or eight years before, when she was still using, when she clung to a relationship with another musician, a talented blues guitarist from St. Paul, for far longer than she should have in hopes of hooking up with the guy permanently. Maybe not in marriage, but at least by living together, by settling down and establishing some semblance of a normal, happy, domestic life. Her vision for them included a kid or two, miniature human beings that were to bring fulfillment for her as a woman.

Beau Dunsmoor, the guitarist, had been her last great romance. Their lovemaking, while not always perfect, had worked. For him. For her. For awhile. Not long after they split up and she moved back to Duluth, where she'd gone to school, she crashed into a significant depression, a condition she deepened by drinking straight vodka and smoking hashish. Her gigs became stagnant pools of uninspired insignificance. Her performances were reduced to mere steady work, economic efforts to generate cash for more booze, more drugs. It took a friend, the female owner of a nightclub in Superior, Wisconsin, a classmate from college, to make Amy confront her addictions.

Coming out of rehab, Amy Maddox expected sex and fulfillment to be as easy as they'd always been. After fits and starts with an assortment of partners, none serious, all relatively nice guys, the singer realized that without the loosening of her internal strings that chemicals provided, she was unable to achieve satisfaction. This recognition hit her hard; it drove her back into the clutches of her demons. She relapsed when she became convinced that alcohol and drugs could re-set her internal compass. But she knew all along that using was going to kill her. She went back into a program on her own. This time, she stayed straight.

"Similar story," she replied after an extended period of silence. "I came up here from Torrance, California to go to school. Took one trip into the Boundary Waters and fell in love with the place."

"Where'd you go to college?" Bill asked, sipping lightly on ice water.

"University of Minnesota, Duluth. Music major. I hope it shows," she added through a significant grin.

The singer felt an increased weariness behind her smile. A deflated texture forced its way into the conversation. Her melancholy didn't seem to bother Bill.

They ate big breakfasts and drank thick coffee beneath a canopy of tobacco haze. If Amy's cigarette smoking annoyed her companion, he didn't let on. The eggs and bacon went down easily. She was hungry from the hard work of performing on the road and from the disappointing angst of her failed attempt at self-gratification in the shower. Amy Maddox studied Bill Martin across the ceramic surface of the table, questioning the wisdom of further encouraging the man.

"What do you have planned for the rest of the morning?" the botanist asked.

"Not much. I need to practice some. I play again tonight at eight."

"I was going to come back and catch your show again. I especially liked that tune about castles in Normandy."

"That's one I borrowed from Lucy Kaplansky though I don't think she wrote it."

"I love her stuff," Bill advised. "She's got such an unusual voice. It melds the East Coast with the Midwest, fuses them together in an unexpected union."

There's substance to this guy, the musician thought. *He invests a lot of thought and insight into relatively short sentences.*

The woman longed to get to know her companion in a more personal context. Fear loomed large behind that contemplation, a fear so delicate and fragile that it lingered covertly beneath every word she uttered.

"Wow. I didn't realize you were a folk groupie," she offered.

"I've seen her a couple of times. She's great. But you know what?"

There was another delay in their interchange. Amy Maddox anticipated what was coming. There would likely issue a comparison of her own art with that of Lucy Kaplansky. Lucy had a recording contract. She wrote movie scores and soundtracks. Amy Maddox had two insignificant self-produced CD's of original music to her credit; albums that had sold a few thousand copies each. Bill from Grand Marais would be making a terrible mistake by attempting a comparison between a folk legend and the woman sitting in front of him with egg yolk on her chin.

"I think you're original," he began. "There's a natural underlying current of unrest, of emotional turmoil behind your lyrics that most other singer-songwriters are forced to construct. The words to your songs don't seem contrived or artificial. The lyrics seem to write themselves. Not that you don't have to work at it. I write some myself. I know how hard it is to put words and music together and make them seem unique. Your songs feel like they're created out of whole cloth. There's great mystery behind craft like that."

Smoke rose above her yellow hair and caught the morning sun. She found herself unable to respond to the compliment. Instead, she merely pulled hard on the tobacco and allowed a melancholy smile to slide across her lips.

"Want to go for a walk?" he asked after they'd returned to lighter conversation and drained several pots of coffee.

"Sure."

Outside the restaurant, she continued to ponder his analysis of her art. Bill walked effortlessly beside her, his bare hands shoved deep into the back pockets of his Levi's, his cap pulled tight to his head against the breeze blowing in off the ice pack. They walked quietly through the village, casting furtive glances at each other. Their pace seemed natural, as if they'd traveled many roads together.

"You said you write some," she said. "What kind of stuff?"

"I plunk around on an old twelve string. I'd love to be able to write and play like you do."

A broad grin erupted across Amy's mouth.

"Practice, Bill. Practice."

"Oh, I do plenty of that, Ms. Maddox. Believe me, I do. But there's more to playing a guitar and writing good music than merely spending time. I don't have your creative bent. I can emulate others well enough. Play songs that others have written and do a passable job of it. But that's where my talent ends."

Their path took them through Grand Marais. Unexpectedly, the singer found herself back in front of her rental cabin.

"How did you know where I was staying?" she asked as they stopped in front of the cottage.

"In this town? Come on. It's impossible for a single woman to remain anonymous in Grand Marais."

"Hadn't thought of it that way," she responded through a slight giggle. "Guess it does get pretty lonely up here for all your unmarried guys."

"I do just fine," Bill answered, looking intently at the woman.

She detected a slight crack in the man's perfection; a brief moment where she'd caught handsome Bill with his guard down. His boast didn't diminish her appreciation of him: it merely confirmed his humanity.

"I'll bet you do. I'd ask you in for coffee but I'm afraid I'm fresh out of filters. Mrs. Eustice, the caretaker, promised to bring me some more. Since I'm headed back to Duluth tomorrow, there doesn't really seem much point in it."

"I'll take a rain check," he replied. There was a steady glow to Bill Martin's cheeks as he looked into her eyes. "It was great talking to you. I'll be there tonight. Maybe we can go out after the show."

Amy's own face, already pink from the cold, began to redden. Desire, primitive and original, colored her cheeks as she struggled with how to end their conversation. A kiss would be too forward; a handshake, too noncommittal. She leaned into the man and gave him a slight hug.

"That'd be nice. Thanks for the morning, Bill. I'll watch for you tonight," she said as she turned to enter her room. "Don't disappoint me," she added in a near whisper.

"I won't," the young man responded. "I wouldn't miss it for the world."

Inside the cottage, Amy stood quietly behind the folds of tightly drawn curtains, the cheap cloth musty with age, and watched William Martin amble down a poorly shoveled sidewalk towards the lake. A sense of intense longing overwhelmed her mind and draped her soul in anxiety. Her right hand reached urgently for her battered guitar. She sat on the edge of the distressed davenport and began to strum the instrument.

Cloaked in morning light filtered by decaying drapes, wonder came over the woman. Lyrics materialized from hidden crevices in Amy Maddox's mind as her fingers struggled to recall a forgotten melody.

FUNERAL FOR A FAT WOMAN

Kyle Larson walked with his head bowed through light drizzle towards a church. The brim of his felt cowboy hat dripped rain. Thick gray-black clouds hung low over the streets of the town. A wind swirled out of the west driving before it the nearly invisible rain.

Larson carried the latest issue of *The Star*, the town's weekly newspaper, in his right hand. Ink seeped from the rolled up newsprint and stained the cuff of his white dress shirt. Even though he hadn't lived in his hometown for many years, Larson still had the paper mailed to him. He wasn't sure why, given his reluctance to cherish the past or recall stale memories.

It was autumn. The rain carried with it a realization of winter. As Kyle moved, his cowboy boots disturbed a carpet of dead leaves deposited on the sidewalk. Debris rose from the pavement, becoming briefly suspended by the wind, only to drift back to the ground as he passed by.

He was in town on a Saturday. Orchard Street, the burg's main thoroughfare, was totally deserted. Many of the storefronts were empty. Wholesale milk prices were at an all time low. Scores of family dairy farms had ceased to operate. Bad times for local farmers meant a similar fate for many local merchants. Larson considered himself lucky: there was a certain machismo in being able to claim that he no longer called this unhappy little place his home.

St. Agnes Catholic Church defined the far end of Orchard Street. The building stood in a place where town ended and country began. The sanctuary's bell tower was the tallest structure for miles. The steeple's white exterior stood in stark contrast to the diminished yellow of the surrounding cornfields. The church itself was clad in lap siding made of fir painted the same brilliant white as the bell tower.

Larson ambled past a cluster of old cars and rusting pick-up trucks parked in a gravel lot next to St. Agnes. Strains of music drifted towards him. He could not make out the tune. But then, he was an agnostic and not prone to recalling the melodies of religious hymns.

Being inside the chapel unnerved him. Kyle walked quickly past the guest book without signing his name. Out of habit, habit long since relegated to memory, the man removed his hat before sitting in the rear-most pew of the church. He placed the soggy fedora on the oak bench next to him and shook the rain out of his limp black hair. Larson absent-mindedly pulled the newspaper out of his coat pocket, opened it to the last page, the page with the hog and cattle prices and the obituaries, and studied the funeral notices.

Music resonated. The song seemed to be a slow, dreary version of *Ave Maria.* Or perhaps not. Perhaps it was something else entirely. Larson lifted his eyeglasses from the bridge of his nose and wiped the lenses with a linen handkerchief. At fifty, he needed his spectacles for everything. Without them, he couldn't see the altar, the priest, or the casket. He replaced the ungainly rims on his nose and counted the mourners. There were less than thirty people in attendance. Even in the closeness of the small church, the place seemed empty.

Larson's eyes strayed from the ceremony in front of him and resumed his scrutiny of the obituaries.

Her name was Arlene Albertson. According to the newspaper, she died at a hospice in Mankato, Minnesota. She died after a "courageous battle with pancreatic cancer." Arlene left behind two daughters and a son. There was no mention of a husband. For some reason, the absence of a husband disturbed him. Arlene's fate seemed unfair; it was unjust in the sense that she didn't have a partner beside her when she died. The obit didn't contain a photograph. He was thankful for the omission.

Kyle Larson closed his exhausted eyes and ignored the priest's incantations. An odor of incense assaulted him. He tried not to inhale the religion.

"Promise me you'll write to me," she had said.

Arlene sat in his lap in the front passenger's seat of his International Scout. She was naked. So was he. Even upon reflection, she was not beautiful. Arlene Albertson was heavy-set with huge fatty breasts. Deep blue veins punctuated the chalk-white skin of her tits. He remembered that her nipples were incredibly small considering the amount of flesh surrounding them. She didn't look anything like the women that haunted him from within the pages of *Playboy* and *Penthouse* that he studied so carefully throughout his adolescence.

Decades of time evaporated. The smell of stale cigarette smoke, perfume, and passion found him in the church pew across an endless meadow of years.

"I promise," he had whispered, knowing that he had no intention of writing to her.

They were in his car in the parking lot of Benson's Tap, a three-two-beer joint outside of town. They shared ten minutes of excitement. He tried not to expand the lie. He didn't make any claim that he loved her. He had no desire to begin a courtship with a fat girl. It was only a brief interlude; a moment spent together a long, long time ago. She was his first. He wasn't hers. She gave him a gift. She made love to Kyle Larson because he was going to 'Nam. She made love to him because he was a virgin and because he was going off to die. They both knew Arlene would wait forever for the promised letter.

It was the damn war that killed God for Kyle Larson. When he came back from Vietnam, he came back to a world incapable of redemption. Arlene had moved. His old buddies teased him, told him that he should find and marry the woman. He married another girl instead, an intelligent, attractive college student from another town. They had two kids and some good years.

Then things went sour. Kyle and Cassie divorced. He moved away. His kids were grown and on their own. He saw them every once and awhile, over holidays or on their respective birthdays. His ex-wife was remarried and living in St. Paul. He never found another woman he could love. He lived alone in Warroad, up near the Canadian Border. He tried to forget the things he'd learned in or knew about his hometown. He forgot about Arlene Albertson. Until he read her obituary.

Driving down from Warroad for her funeral, an old Warren Zevon tune came on the radio. He found himself exiting the freeway near Moorhead compelled by words:

We made mad love
Shadow love
Random love
And abandoned love
Accidentally like a martyr
The hurt gets worse and the heart gets harder...

He was stunned to find that the death of someone he'd known so superficially could gnaw at him. He'd witnessed the brutal combat deaths of members of his platoon during the war. He'd seen Vietnamese women and children turned into human torches for no greater offense than looking like the enemy. It was unsettling to discover that the passing of such an ordinary woman could access his emotions.

Her coffin was suspended above the pit. A meager group gathered near the gravesite and shivered in the rain. Two young women and a young man, marginally obese and faintly reminiscent of their mother, stood sobbing in front of the casket. Kyle Larson kept to himself. He remained off to one side watching clear rainwater flow briskly over the polished metal surface of the coffin. A few words, a few tears. People began to depart.

The veteran's hand reached into the folds of his overcoat. He felt foolish. He wanted to be done with his task, done with the old places and the forgotten obligations.

Larson removed a ragged piece of paper from his pocket, exposing the document to the storm. Drops of moisture beat a cadence against timeworn script as the soldier placed the parchment on the damp metal of the casket and began to walk away.

The envelope he left behind was addressed to Arlene. An uncanceled postage stamp was affixed in the appropriate place on the document. He'd carried the letter with him, for no particular reason, or perhaps, for the most particular of reasons, for the better part of his adult life.

The ex-soldier stopped at the edge of the graveyard and looked back across the broad, flat landscape of the Great Plains. His eyes took in the town he'd grown up in and the farm fields he'd left behind. The veteran tried to speak to the Creator, tried desperately to ask God to have mercy on Arlene Albertson's soul but Kyle Larson found that he was no longer able to pray.

THE ENLIGHTMENT OF HOWARD BELL

Night falls quickly in Baudette, Minnesota during the winter. By four o'clock in the afternoon on most January days, evening begins before folks make it home from work. Once the sun settles behind the prairie hills to the west of town, Baudette's minimal streetlights begin to illuminate the way home.

In his late fifties, Judge Howard Bell was a small, wiry man with a shortened gait and ruddy skin. The people of Lake of the Woods County knew him simply as "The Judge". He was the only judge in the county and had been such for over twenty years.

Bell claimed the position of District Court Judge, the trial court level in the Minnesota judicial system, based upon political patronage and a life-long dedication to the Democratic Farmer Labor Party. His rise to power was not the product of a brilliant legal career or a keen mind. Howard Bell's past contained neither. Instead, Judge Bell's fate was tied to the candidate for Governor he supported back in the 1970's. When Howard's candidate won, he won. It was as simple as that.

Heavy snow began to fall. Judge Bell followed an unlit path through a line of trees defining the edge of the town's only park. His house, one of few Victorians in the village, stood as a silent shadow off in the near distance. The neat, crisp lawn of the park was covered with several inches of hard-packed snow, to which the storm was applying a fresh mantle.

Howard's insulated pack boots slid through the lacy texture of the snowfall. He wore an overcoat but no hat. His short gray hair was thick with hair tonic and exposed to the weather. His glasses accumulated white where flakes of snow adhered to the lenses of his bifocals.

Judge Bell was in all ways and in all particulars an undistinguished and ordinary jurist. Baudette had not had a single murder occur during his tenure. Most of

Howard Bell's day-to-day life on the bench dealt with juvenile delinquency, petty thefts, traffic arrests, and family court matters: divorces, child support, alimony, and custody disputes. All in all, the job held little intellectual challenge. Even if such a challenge had been presented, Judge Bell was ill equipped to meet it.

Voices alerted him. There were others in the park. He recognized the tone and the inflection of the speech as Native American. Judge Bell's ears strained to make out the details of the conversation. He tried to locate the source of the disturbance. The woods fell silent save for the sound of falling snow.

"Hey, where do you think you're going?" a voice called out.

A dark form blocked the judge's path. Two other silhouettes stood away from the confrontation. Howard Bell stopped short of the men. Though there was considerable space between them, the judge detected an odor of nervous sweat emanating from the strangers.

"Just on my way home, gentlemen," Bell explained, extending his right hand in greeting. "I'm Judge Bell."

The bigger man made a deliberate step towards Bell. The features of the intruder's face came into focus. Details of the other men remained clouded by the swirling snow and the depleted light. The judge noted that the big man had wide flat nostrils, a square hairless jaw, and long black hair. Howard Bell guessed that the man was Ojibwe.

"You don't even recognize me, do you?" the Indian asked.

The words carried with them a sense of foreboding. No attempt was made to shake the judge's hand. Instead, the Native American kept his own hands firmly anchored in the pockets of a ragged fatigue jacket.

"Should I?" Howard Bell retorted with false skepticism.

"Jackson. Emil Jackson," the stranger said, pointing to a stitched version of his name displayed on the right upper pocket of his jacket.

"Sorry. Should I know you?"

The Indian's companions gained positions on either flank of the judge. Their faces remained concealed. They didn't speak.

"You heard my child custody case and visitation case last week. You took my two daughters away from me. Said I wasn't fit to see them or care for them until I went to dry out and anger management counseling."

Jackson spoke in a steady pattern. There was just a hint of danger in the man's angular face.

"I don't remember that," the judge replied.

In his mind, Judge Bell saw no reason to continue the discussion. He had nothing to apologize for:

"Now if you'll excuse me, I've got to get home for dinner."

Judge Bell began to shuffle forward. A hand gripped the jurist's right shoulder and stopped his progress.

"You ain't leaving until Big Jack says so," one of the other men commanded.

From the characteristics of the assailant's voice it was obvious that at least one of Jackson's companions was also Native American. Bell guessed that the third individual blocking his way home was likely Ojibwe as well.

The judge turned in anger. Jackson stepped in and placed his broad form chest to chest with Howard Bell. The Indian's breath was hot and close. The fear of the unknown began to work at the older man's bowels.

"'We've got other plans for you," Big Jack asserted through a narrow grin.

"Now you see here. I'm a District Court Judge. What you're doing is liable to get you boys in a whole lot of trouble. I'd suggest you step out of the way. You do that and I'll forget that this ever happened," Howard responded with artificial bellicosity.

The judge attempted to harness his emotions but knew his words were soaked in terror. Before he could offer another entreaty, Emil Jackson's right hand hit the little man hard and square on the chin. The blow took Judge Bell by surprise and knocked him down. His eyeglasses flew off from the force of the blow and settled in the snow. Cowering on the ground, Howard raised one arm to defend himself. A boot whipped through the cold air and struck the jurist in the stomach. Blows began to rain down on him from all sides. For a brief moment, Howard Bell flailed away with his ungloved hands in an attempt to deflect the assault. In the end, he failed. His face bloodied and bruised, the judge collapsed onto the unforgiving ground and yielded to his attackers.

They could have killed him right there in the park. They did not. As Howard Bell fought to maintain consciousness, the big Indian leaned down and whispered:

"No one can protect you. Even if you put me away, there are others who'll find you and finish the job. You've pissed off too many of my brothers and sisters over the years for us to let this go any longer. When I come back to court ncxt Monday, I'll expect to see a change of heart."

The Native American studied the terrified face of his adversary before continuing:

"Or you may not have any heart left at all."

The judge didn't reply. His mind concentrated on limiting his pain, on deflecting his humiliation. As the attackers left him, Jackson issued a parting admonition:

"Maybe next time when an Indian speaks in your court, you'll at least make an attempt to listen."

It was the pounding in his head that eventually caused Judge Bell to raise himself out of the snow and stand up. His jaw was tender. His nose was raw. The rapidly falling snow concealed any trace of his spectacles. Blind and humbled, the judge staggered home.

In the stark light of his bathroom, Howard Bell dabbed blood away from his cheeks with a washrag moistened with warm water. Purple bruises were already forming around both of his eyes. The bridge of his nose was obviously broken.

Bell wasn't an intellectual. He barely made it into Gonzaga University Law School with minimally acceptable undergraduate grades. He failed the bar exam the first time he took it. His legal career was largely based upon good luck, luck that included moving to Baudette and finding work with Elmer Johnson. To say that Judge Bell was a contemplative man would be doing a disservice to the deep thinkers of the world.

Johnson was the only lawyer in town during the late 1960's when Howard Bell arrived and took on the role of Elmer Johnson's associate. As the only lawyer north of Bemidji, east of Roseau, and west of International Falls, Elmer Johnson held the position of City Attorney for the City of Baudette at the time and turned all of his municipal work over to his apprentice. It was easy, routine work, well in keeping with Howard's abilities: drafting city ordinances, advising the City Council, and prosecuting petty crimes. The work made Howard Bell visible in the community and connected him with the City Fathers, the police, and the sheriff's department. When Elmer passed away in 1972, Howard Bell became the village's only attorney.

As a child growing up in Des Moines, Iowa, Howard Bell wasn't exposed to Native Americans beyond what he saw at the local Movie Theater or on television. In college and in law school, Indians were few and far between. They seemed to Bell, from his distant point of observation, to be a quiet, unassuming people. When he moved north, his contacts with Native Americans became more frequent. Occasionally, he represented an Ojibwe in court or performed transactional work for an Indian family. He came to Lake of the Woods County without any preconceived bias or prejudice but, soon thereafter, began to follow the lead of his white colleagues in positions of power. He began to stereotype his Indian neighbors in ways that were not kind, and oftentimes, not accurate. Not that Howard Bell realized he was doing this. He was not emotionally constructed to self-evaluate, to analyze his own behavior.

As a District Court Judge, Bell saw Native American people nearly every day he was on the bench. Had he been paying attention, he would have come to understand the socioeconomic reasons behind why they ended up in court before him in disproportionate numbers. But such issues were too complex, too troubling for Howard to spend time on. Stereotypes proved easier and met with a certain acceptance amongst the voting population.

Judge Bell's legs shook as he studied his profile in the lavatory mirror. If he had still been married to Ruth, she would have taken care of him. How had he lost her? Maggie and Elizabeth, their two daughters, were long gone from the house when Ruth finally said she'd had enough. Enough of Howard's late night trips to Melissa Bordridge's place out by Warroad. Enough of his dull wit and inability to empathize. Enough of his plaintive, weak emotions.

As limited as the judge's intellect was, standing in his bathroom beneath the scrutiny of his life, he knew he had caused his marriage to crumble. He couldn't see it at the time, or maybe he just couldn't admit to it until a pissed off Indian beat some sense into him only a few steps from his own front door.

"Shit," Howard Bell whispered as he touched the rough edge of the rag to a deep wound on his forehead.

The jurist examined his reflection. He traced the hard, thin lines that formed the basis of the character of his face with a slightly bent index finger. He touched the moist end of the cloth to the raised skin near his widow's peak and cleaned the abrasion with the washrag. His clothes were a mess. His shirt was ruined, covered in dirt and blood. Pieces of wet bark and leaves clung to the wool of his suit coat and trousers, the black fabric stained with more blood. His thoughts turned from his ex-wife to Emil Jackson.

"What the hell did I do to that crazy asshole? What was that bullshit he said about not listening?"

Judge Bell had no insight into what the Indian meant. Had he, as he commonly did, cut the man short in court? Had he simply adopted the recommendations of the County Social Worker, as he almost always did? How had he wronged the man? The judge didn't know and couldn't begin to remember the specifics of their previous connection.

The big man's features were etched with definiteness in the jurist's mind. Bell knew he would have no trouble picking the man out of a mug book or a lineup. Howard was the victim of a felony level assault. A conviction would mean that at Jackson would do prison time. But why had the assault occurred? Why had Jackson erupted? What had Howard Bell done but follow the law, order the standard limitations in a situation where parents are alcoholic and unable to control their tempers?

Try as he might, the judge had a difficult time placing Emil Jackson as an individual case. There was a slight inkling, a minor recollection of the man being in front of Judge Bell in the recent past, but nothing more. The Ojibwe was lost in a sea of unremarkable, indistinguishable Indians that had come before Howard Bell over the decades he'd served on the District Court. Judge Bell decided not to go to the police. He did not go to the County Attorney. It wasn't out of some epiphany of intellect that he remained silent. It was out of self-preservation.

While it was true that one word from Bell would have been sufficient to lock up Jackson for a good long time, prison would not end the nightmare. There were others, just as the big Native American had said, with grudges to bare against the jurist, others who would take up Emil Jackson's torch. And Howard Bell had no idea who they were.

Certainly Judge Bell knew Jackson's buddies were Native American and likely Ojibwe. Beyond that, and the fact that both of the accomplices were small in stature, Howard Bell was unable to call to mind any details of the other two men. It made abundant sense to Judge Bell, when all of the evidence was considered, to simply forget that the incident had ever taken place.

Emil Jackson's matter did not come before Judge Bell during the following week. For some reason, the child custody matter was transferred to another county. Bell never inquired as to why. It may have been that the mother of Jackson's children moved away. It may have been that child support and collections transferred the file to collect back support from Jackson at some new job in another venue. Whatever the reason, Howard Bell never crossed paths with the big Indian again.

Despite this lack of contact, Judge Bell had no difficulty recalling the hard, angry features of the Native American whenever the jurist tried to fall asleep in his big house on the banks of the Rainy River. And during the months that followed the attack, Howard Bell thought he recognized Emil Jackson's voice whenever an Ojibwe person addressed Judge Bell in the courtroom. It was only a short period of time before Howard Bell began to listen.

IDA'S LAST CHRISTMAS

Her eyes hung heavy with age. Who could blame her? Ida Undenberg had outlived her husband, her siblings, and all her children. At ninety-five, she could no longer see well enough to leave her apartment in the East End of Duluth. Her ears were so poor that she had trouble hearing the grocery boy knock on her door when he announced a delivery. Her legs and back had become twisted and useless with arthritis. But her spirit raged on.

How many Christmas seasons had passed since Herbert died? Twenty? Twenty-one? Her memory failed her as to such details, details that no longer meant anything. The birch runners of Ida's chair rocked uneasily across the linoleum floor. A thin film of cooking grease muffled the sound of wood striking floor. An old timepiece on the wall counted the seconds and reminded the old woman that life itself was a brief and fleeting exercise. The clock's intricate pace reflected a pattern distinctly at odds with the rhythm of the rocking chair.

Cold chicken sat on her plate. Mashed potatoes, the gravy long since grown cold and congealed, surrounded the business end of a spoon. The woman's gnarled fingers rested in her lap. Blue veins protruded from both hands and betrayed her age. She couldn't finish her Christmas Eve dinner. Loneliness occupied her innards, filling her up with the past. Ida rested uncomfortably on the cushion of her chair, tilted her head back, and slowly closed her eyes.

Clouds filled the North Dakota sky. Heavy weather rolled in across the prairie. Caught out in the storm, a girl, wet from descending rain, ducked into Undenberg's barn. She leaned her bicycle against the impoverished wood of the interior of the structure. Water dripped from the bike's metal frame. Ida was used to being alone. She was the youngest of seven children. Storms didn't frighten her. Harsh weather empowered her with a sense of awe.

God lives in a North Dakota storm, she thought to herself as she studied the swirling clouds through the open barn door.

The girl rested on a wooden bench just inside the entrance to the building. She didn't see Herbert Undenberg, two years older than her at fifteen, sneak up from behind.

""Hey," the lanky boy shouted, as if yelling "boo", lightly touching the top of Ida's shoulder, startling her.

"God, you scared me," she exclaimed.

"Sure is somethin', isn't it?" he remarked, pointing to the churning sky and torrential downpour.

Absently, the boy sat down next to her on the bench. She was comfortable sitting alongside Herbert Undenberg on that occasion. She understood at that moment that she'd always be comfortable next to him. Herbert wasn't as handsome as some. He was a little thin, a little too raw-boned. But his heart was big and pure. He trusted God. More importantly, their union came to evince a great friendship. They would weather horrendous events and experience occasions of great jubilation over the course of fifty years of their marriage to each other.

There was a knock at the door.

"Mrs. Undenberg?" a small voice inquired.

The old woman had trouble deciphering the words. She leaned forward in her chair. Her eyes opened with the patience of great age. With supreme effort, Ida stood up and began the long journey to the door. The widow placed her right hand along the kitchen wall to support herself as she shuffled forward.

"Coming," she replied.

The prospect of a visitor brightened the widow's outlook. Once at the door, Ida fumbled with the deadbolt. Because the voice outside her door seemed familiar, she didn't bother to look through the peephole before opening the door. As the panel swung inward, the three Morgan children appeared illumined by decadent light. Amy, thirteen-years-old, blond and pretty; Adam, ten, dark eyed and full of mischief; and Angela, five, petite and bashful, waited for an invitation to enter Ida's apartment.

"Merry Christmas, ma'am," the oldest Morgan child offered.

Amy handed the woman a basket of fresh fruit, the kind sold ready-made in the grocery stores. A smile swept across the wrinkled cheeks of Ida Undenberg at the sight of the gift.

"Come in, come in," she commanded in a soft voice.

The Morgan's lived in a two-room flat next door. Their mother, April, was single, trying to raise the kids on her own. There was no evidence of a father. Ida speculated that April must have decided the Morgan children would fare better with a stable mother than a set of squabbling parents. The mystery of the father's absence allowed the old woman to conjure up any number of similar suppositions, none of which Ida ever shared with April Morgan. In the old woman's view, her neighbor was doing a fine job of rearing children and there was no reason for further dialogue on the subject.

The widow reached for the fruit and grabbed the basket by its wicker handle. As her fingers wrapped around the fibers, her left arm sagged under the weight of the gift.

"Adam help her with that," Amy whispered.

The boy glared at his sister. He was not keen on the critical tone used by his older sibling. Adam muttered but complied, carrying the offering into the old woman's apartment, depositing it on the table next to her half-eaten dinner.

"Thank you Adam," Mrs. Undenberg said. "Do you want an apple or banana to take along with you?"

114

"No thanks," Adam responded. "We gotta get back an' open presents."

"On Christmas Eve? What about Santa?" she asked, looking kindly at Angela, the youngest Morgan child.

"There's no Santy Claus," the little girl related in a serious voice. "Darla Knutsen told me it's momma who buys all the presents."

The old woman stared for a long time at the wide blue eyes and cherubic face of the child, all the while wondering how little ones became so wise, so fast.

"Please thank your mother for me, will you?"

"Sure thing, Mrs. Undenberg. Have a Merry Christmas," Amy added, closing the door behind the departing children.

Ida left the fruit basket and the dishes on the table. Her eyes studied the plastic limbs of her artificial Christmas tree. There had been a time when she and Herbert put up Norway pines and blue spruce in the living room of their farmhouse near Mille Lacs Lake in Central Minnesota: trees cut from their own land that stood twenty-feet-high. The woman's eyes were drawn away from the falsity of the meager tree standing on top of her television. Her gaze became riveted on the weather. A winter storm was approaching. The widow lumbered cautiously to the window.

"Herbert," she called quietly.

Ida squinted. Straining her eyes, she looked through foggy glass at the street below her apartment. She searched for her husband along the sidewalks and in the alleys, searched for him in the swirling snow and the bitter cold of the Christmas Eve storm. She knew he was out there, somewhere, waiting for her.

FAITH

Sister Mary Francis Franklin sits on the edge of her bed. A fragrance of perfumed skin lotion drifts across the Spartan confines of her room. Her eyes are open and focused on the cold bluestone walls of her living space. The woman's mind is distant, contemplatively so. A white envelope rests in her lap. The seal is carefully broken. The glued edges of the flap are trim, revealing the precision with which the nun opened the parcel. An old fashioned wind-up alarm clock occupies the top of an antique nightstand next to the Sister's bed. The mechanical sound of the timepiece seems to foretell the rhythm of the woman's breathing. Her small white hands lightly touch the envelope. Nervous fingers trace and retrace her name and address on the paper. There is no return address.

She knows. From the handwriting on the envelope, she knows. Her inner self cries as she clutches the missive. Though no tears fall, her face reflects soulful anguish. She recalls the last time she saw the handwriting. The neat printing has become a catalyst of upset in her cloistered world. Her meditative powers seem to fail her. She cannot, as she forces her gaze upon the cruel stones of the floor, forget. She can only remember.

"Hi. I'm Donny, Donny James."
His voice had been deep, manly and assertive.
"Mary Frankowiak," she had whispered in response, her voice passive and shy.
He was tall, of slender build, ample red hair and fragile, feminine cheekbones. His skin, as she remembered it, was milky white, far whiter than her own. He wore a Bluegolds letter jacket. It was 1976. The bright gold numerals stitched on soft faded blue calfskin haunt her across time. He was a star forward on the University of Wisconsin-Eau Claire basketball team. That

116

fact had impressed her, though she believed she was beyond such high school foolishness. They met in the serenity of the university library.

"Whatcha readin'?" Donny had asked as he'd leaned over Mary and brushed her thick black hair off her shoulder.

The boy scrutinized the cover of the book in front of him.

"*Victory* by Joseph Conrad," she responded in uncertain words.

"Never heard of it. Sounds like a war story."

Her mind, even now, years removed from the moment, remembers the curiosity in his voice. Even from memory, his inquiry seems genuine.

"Nope. It's about a man on an island and a woman he meets."

"I'd call that false advertising," he chirped. "Title makes it sound like a war story."

He had displayed a healthy smile as they conversed.

"I haven't seen you around her before. You must be a freshman," he said.

She laughed. She was a senior just like him. After four years on campus, he'd finally noticed her. She calculated that his sudden interest in her was due to the fact that she'd recently changed from glasses to contact lenses and had updated her hairstyle. She'd seen Donny James countless times in the halls and on the basketball court during varsity games. He was a star. She knew that about him the first week she was on campus.

Sitting in the austerity of her room, she recalls his hand brushing lightly against the soft fabric of her sweater in the hollow just between her breasts. The gesture had caused her breath to falter. She thought, at the time, that it was an inculpable coincidence. Now, manipulating the crispness of the envelope, she questions his intent.

"How'd you like to go to the Couple's Dance with me this Friday?" he'd asked, his voice coarse and deep.

The words had fallen softly and caused a stir inside her. The young woman's response had been limited to an affirmative nod of the head.

"Great. You in the women's dorms?"

Another nod.

"I'll be by around seven. See you then."

Just as swiftly as he'd materialized, Donny James vanished, melting into the crush of students surging through the hallways.

"Donny James? Are you serious?" Sharon Hedstrom had queried, staring at Mary Francis in utter disbelief.

Sharon was her roommate at the time. Immediately after receiving the news, the round-faced co-ed began a search of her closet for a low cut gown that would embolden her friend. Sharon was slightly taller than Mary Francis was. The roommate's blond hair was cropped short, making the curve of her jaw and cheeks seem exaggerated. Green mascara perpetually argued with Sharon's nearly pigmentless eyes. The make-up was distinctly unnatural against her Nordic skin.

"When was the last time you went to a dance?" Sharon asked

Mary Francis sat on the edge of her bed searching her memory for an answer. Her ravenesque mane was held in place by a single red ribbon.

"Last summer. For French Club."

"That wasn't a dance. That was a dirge. I mean a wild, let-it-all-hang-out dance?"

"I don't know."

The nun's attention drifts towards the image of Donny James retained by her mind. His reflection in her memory causes her to sigh.

Sharon ultimately liberated a dress from her clothes collection.

"This should catch his eye," her roommate had remarked. "Try it on."

Mary Francis pulled her sweatshirt over her head, unbuttoned her jeans, and stepped free of the denim. Standing in her underwear, she coaxed the dress past her waist. Carefully threading each arm through the gown's ethereal straps, she smoothed the fabric until the garment was an undisturbed, seamless piece of black. The silk pressed tightly against her hips. The nearly invisible straps accentuated her delicate neck and shoulders.

"This will catch his eye for sure," Mary Francis acknowledged.

She danced every dance with him. With each turn of the floor, she felt more loved. The strength of his arms made her feel secure. They didn't speak as they revolved around the floor. The magic of the music swept them away, to someplace far from Eau Claire, Wisconsin. The melody stopped. Bright lights came on. The illumination hurt their eyes. As the crowd began to move towards the doors, he spoke:

"Some of us are going to Lisa Good's. Wanna come along?"

"Who's Lisa Good?" she asked.

"You sure don't get out much, do you? Lisa Good has the greatest parties in town. Her dad runs Good-Hayes Motors, the Chevy dealer. She has her own '75 'Vette."

As they left the dance, something alarmed her. Surreptitiously, she cast a sidelong glance at her date. His facial expression seemed kind and decent. Her concern passed.

"OK, just as long as we don't stay too late," she replied.

Her response was hesitant. Though she was excited that Donny wanted the evening to continue, that he found her worthy of his company, she did not wish to appear overly impressed.

"Sure, anything you say."
The Good Mansion was full of college kids dancing to the Doobie Brothers. The words to *China Grove* reverberated off the walls of the formal living room.

"What's that?" she asked pointing to a glass of amber liquor in Donny's right hand.

"180 Proof Jamaican Rum. You gotta drink it down quick or it'll kill you."

The basketball star snatched another glass of rum off a nearby counter.

"Here," he urged through a charismatic smile as he handed her the tumbler.

"I don't drink."

"Why not?"

"I just don't."

"You're ready to graduate from college and you don't drink?"

"That's right.'

"Ah, come on. Just one little sip. If you don't like it, I'll toss it in the sink."

Donny James' eyes had narrowed. His voice had taken on an unfamiliar edge, an edge similar to the tone that had earlier caused her mild concern.

"I said I don't drink. Look, Donny, I had a great time at dinner and at the dance but maybe it's time to go," she offered timidly.

"Sure. Anything you say. I just want to show you something before we leave."

"What's that?"

"Lisa's got the neatest rec room you've ever seen. It's downstairs. Come on."

His hand tightened around her wrist as he led her through the crowd. The strength of his grip was unnatural. She tried to think. She looked around. There was no one in the house that she really knew. The people were all Donny's clique, his friends. She yielded to the pressure of his advance and followed the young man against her better judgment. The basement recreation room was bathed in soft illumination. Once he convinced her to follow him into Lisa's downstairs bedroom, the subterfuge was complete. The basement's elusive lighting did little to lessen the brutality of the rape.

Her hands tremble as she holds the envelope. She remembers the slow, ugly moments of that night as she holds the message. She has no trouble recalling the event. The bitter seed of Donny James' harvest, the reality of her shame, hasn't lessened over time. She left the university. She did not return the tattered remnants of the borrowed dress to Sharon. She blamed no one but herself. Her virginity was stolen from her because she ignored her instincts and foolishly accompanied Donny James into the basement that night.

She transferred to another state college and completed her degree. Before leaving Eau Claire, she learned she was pregnant. She revealed her secret to her roommate because Sharon had previously experienced an unwanted pregnancy. Mary Francis trusted that Sharon could maintain a confidence. She was wrong. Somehow, Donny James learned about her condition. For two years, he sent letter after letter to Mary Francis. She never opened the envelopes. The correspondence stopped once she changed her last name to "Franklin" and entered the Benedictine Order in Duluth, Minnesota.

"Mary, the Bishop is waiting on you."
Sister Barbara's voice disturbs the past. Barbara is short, thick of mind, and elderly, with glasses that remain miraculously in place against the extreme pitch of her nose. Despite these traits, Mary has a fondness for Sister Barbara.
"I'm coming. Give me a minute, will you?"
"You don't want to keep Bishop Inglimo waiting. My, how we've waited for this day. How can you stand it?

121

I mean, the pressure and all? It'd kill me to be in your shoes."

The young nun turns away so that the older woman cannot see her tears.

"I'll stall them for a minute or two. But please hurry. You need to get dressed and get out there for your big day," Sister Barbara urges.

Mary rises to her feet, opens the envelope, and withdraws a single sheet of photocopy paper, a duplicate of a medical record, from inside. The document describes a first trimester abortion. The nun places the paperwork in the top drawer of her desk. The handwriting on the most recent envelope is identical to cursive adorning a stack of old mail already secreted in the desk.

Sister Mary Francis removes her clothing. Her hands shake as she unhooks her bra. Placing the wired garment and the habit on the bed, the nun steps free of her underpants. Bending at the waist, Mary picks the panties up, and lays them on the bed with the other clothing. Her bare feet pad noiselessly to the door. Her fingers draw the latch. Pivoting on her heels, she retreats across the rough stone floor to the bathroom. A solid gold chain and crucifix encircles her neck. The jewelry bounces against her bare sternum as she moves. The gentle curves of her chest shift with the pattern of her gait. Her skin measures the coldness of the room.

Kneeling before a bathtub, she turns on the water. Steam rises from the cold porcelain. When the tub is full, she turns off the faucet. Biting her tongue against the heat, she enters scalding water. Pain causes her to lose her breath. Her buttocks and legs turn crimson.

A tired breath escapes her lips. Mary Francis leans against the back of the tub and rests her head on a clean white terrycloth towel. Her hair is shorter now and turns limp from the steam. Her hands massage the muscles of her upper arms and her calves. She touches the softness of her lips. Both hands come to rest upon the crucifix. Her eyes close. She makes the sign of the cross above her naked body. A hand reaches out in search of the instrument.

The violence of the act surprises her. It's as if someone else is drawing the straight razor across her larynx. The blade is very sharp. She feels no pain, although the suddenness of the blood frightens her. Panicking, she seeks to undo the deed. Her hands tighten around her throat in an attempt to close off the wound. But the cut is too deep, the edge of the blade, too exquisite. She cannot turn back. She cannot deny the inevitable conclusion of her sin. A breeze finds a crack in the stone wall behind a window frame. Rose colored waves lap at Mary Francis' body as the nun slips into unconsciousness.

In the adjacent room, a newspaper clipping, freshly cut and pinned to a bulletin board, flutters in the migrating draft. The article hanging above the nun's desk announces that Bishop Inglimo has chosen this day to ordain Sister Mary Francis Franklin as the first woman priest in the Roman Catholic Church.

REUNION

"Who's that?" Jimmy Mancetti asked, gesturing at an attractive woman in her forties sitting alone across the dance floor.

Mancetti was seated with four women. One dark haired beauty wore a gold miniskirt revealing the full extent of her deeply muscled legs. The other brunette in the group was dressed in black slacks and a black top, her satin blouse purposefully left open at the second button, displaying a hint of cleavage.

Next to the brunette in the pantsuit, a diminutive redhead, her skin pale, the color of pasteurized milk, methodically stirred a gin and tonic. At the far end of the table a tall sensuous blond fingered a long stemmed glass half full of white zinfandel.

"You'll never guess", teased the redhead.

"Come on, Gina, give me a hint."

"Arf, arf," the dark one in the miniskirt barked.

"What the hell is that all about?"

"Gaines Burgers, Jimmy. You remember Gaines Burgers, don't you?" Diane, the blond, whispered.

Mancetti cast a puzzled glance at the woman across the room. He studied her features under the reduced light of the dance hall. A tangle of thickly curled brown hair was tied up off the woman's neck. Her skin was flawless; her form appeared slender and supple beneath the brilliant blue of her sleeveless dress as she sipped a drink and absently watched couples slow dance to Clapton's *You Are Wonderful Tonight*.

Beyond her, on top of a well-worn stage, a DJ stood behind a bank of equipment searching his CD collection for a song someone had requested.

"Still don't know who she is?" Beth, the redhead, asked.

Jimmy looked away from the mystery woman.

"Beth, I haven't got a fucking clue."

Restrained laughter rose in unison from around the table. The women giggled in predatory, superior fashion. They were used to Jimmy Mancetti having the upper hand by virtue of his keen wit, bitter sarcasm, and well-rehearsed put-downs of the mundane and the ordinary. Obtaining an advantage over Mancetti was a rare event, a moment to be savored.

April, one of the dark haired women, struggled against the fabric of her miniskirt as she leaned across the table:

"That's Gloria DeSmedt, you idiot."

The man returned his eyes to the distant woman.

"No way. That's about half of Gloria."

"She lost her husband, you remember, Gus Tucker, that retarded farm kid?" April added.

Jimmy studied the female sitting near the edge of darkness. Gus Tucker had not been retarded. He wore the brand of a "retard" at school because he was a klutz and a below average student. Mancetti never really had anything against Gus. Still, Tucker had always been an easy target for Mancetti's unkind sarcasm in the hallways of MacGregor High School.

"Gloria and Gus' farm went belly up about ten years ago. They moved to Brainerd. I hear they lived in a basement apartment, a real dive. He took a job as a mechanic. Then he had a heart attack. When he died, she completely lost it. His mom has the kids. She's been waitressing and hitting the bars pretty hard ever since," April advised.

Above them, strung between the walls of the MacGregor VFW, a hand-lettered banner proclaimed the reason for the gathering:

"Welcome Mercs! MacGregor High School Class of '73".

"She doesn't look anything like she did in high school," Jimmy observed.

"Duh. Do any of us?"

Mancetti ignored Gina. He was lost in the memory of the singular cruelty he'd perpetrated against Gloria DeSmedt nearly thirty years ago.

He always considered her one of the least interesting girls in MacGregor. Since there were so few kids in his class, he knew her from grade school on. She was quiet, uninvolved in sports or school activities. She had been, in all ways, distinctly different from the four former cheerleaders he was sitting with at the reunion.

Gloria was someone he'd say a perfunctory "hello" to in the halls. He was a town kid. She was a farm girl. They had nothing in common. Nothing brought them together until she asked him to the Sweetheart Dance during the winter of their senior year.

Jimmy and Beth had just broken up. It was over the usual stuff. He wanted to bone her in the back of his dad's 1969 Grand Prix Station wagon. Beth wanted a commitment. He'd been with just about every other girl in their class, one way or another. Beth LeGarde was the last one on his "list". Her not-so-subtle rejection of Mancetti's advances put an abrupt end to his quest to add her name to his personal score sheet.

Jimmy hadn't been a jock and he wasn't all that handsome. But he was cool; cool because he played lead guitar in the town's only garage band. He was also cool because he had unlimited access to pot and booze through his older brother Dennis, a perennial freshman at St. Cloud State.

The football players liked Jimmy. The basketball players liked Jimmy. It was a natural progression that, hanging around with jocks, Mancetti did all right with the cheerleaders.

Beth LeGarde told Jimmy to fuck himself when he wouldn't stop pulling at the zipper of her jeans in the back of the Pontiac. She slapped him hard when his hand dove underneath her sweater. Her rejection left him with his periscope unceremoniously distended. By the next day, it was all over school that they'd broken up. That's when Gloria DeSmedt approached him.

"Hi."

"Hey, what's happening, Gloria?"

"I heard you and Beth had a fight."

"Yup. She told me to take a hike, though not quite in those words."

"That's sad."

"It's probably for the best. What's up?"

He remembered looking away from her because he found her uninteresting. Her face wasn't ugly. In fact, in hindsight, he recalled her face was pleasant enough. She had quick brown eyes and clean skin. It was her body that turned him off. Not that she was enormous. She was just a little on the heavy side. But in comparison to the lithe, lean forms of the girls he preferred, the distinction was significant.

"The Sweetheart's in two weeks," she had said in a timid voice.

"So?"

He'd begun to guess why the less than perfect Gloria DeSmedt was standing in front of his locker extending their normally curt politeness into an awkward personal conversation.

"Well..."

There was a long pause as she gathered the courage to ask him.

"Would you go to the Dance with me?"

Mancetti watched the woman he'd once known as Gloria DeSmedt walk across the VFW auditorium towards the bar. She flowed with a grace and suggestiveness that she'd never displayed as a girl. Gloria had not only slimmed down. She'd grown up.

"Are you out of your fucking mind?"

He'd walked away from her, ending their discussion about the Sweetheart Dance with calculated

127

enmity. A few days later, Andy Swenson and Pete Johnson, captains of the basketball team and his best friends, brought him a gift during fourth period, their lunch hour.

"We heard you're taking Gloria DeSmedt to the Sweetheart."

"Yeah, right. And the US Army's going to win the Vietnam War."

"Open it up."

Johnson's face broke into a wide, evil grin as he handed a brown lunch sack to Mancetti. Inside the bag, the guitar player found two Gaines Burgers: dog food.

Despite the private nature of the joke, Mancetti's mind unreasonably magnified the impact of the prank on his reputation. At least that's how he remembered it happening. When Gloria DeSmedt entered the lunchroom that day, instinct took over.

"Gloria, I brought you something."

He'd smiled and swung his lanky form over a chair next to her. She was sitting at a lunch table with three of her friends, girls that Jimmy never took notice of, much less talked to.

"What is it?"

"It's a surprise. I felt bad about the way I treated you."

"Really"

"Open it," he said, handing her the sack containing the dog food.

For a few days after the incident, her anguish bothered Mancetti, though once he found a date for the dance, he didn't give Gloria DeSmedt another thought.

The DJ placed another CD in the changer.

"I'm going to go ask her to dance."

"You can't be serious," Gina said.

"You guys are all married and boring. I'm single. She's single. What's the harm in asking?"

"She'll probably knock you on your ass, you sanctimonious bastard," Beth added through a cackle.

"Maybe. But then, I deserve it, don't I?"

Mancetti stood up and smoothed the khaki fabric of his Dockers. His well-tanned arms contrasted with the brilliant yellow sleeves of his golf shirt. He made his way through the crowd with confidence.

"Can I buy you a drink?"

She turned towards him. Jimmy was unprepared for his reaction. She was pretty. The baby fat of her youth was gone, replaced by a rare face. Age had made her more attractive, not less. Time had added character to her formerly nondescript features. Her brown eyes stared at him with quiet calm. He furtively scanned her body, cloaked as it was in a slight shimmer of blue. Her chest was ample and discernible against the tight fit of the fabric. She was far more sensual than he remembered. It was an amazing transformation.

"Hi," she responded.

"Buy you a drink?"

He didn't enunciate the words with the level of assurance that he'd expected.

"Sure. I'm drinking Long Island Teas," she replied.

"Two of those knock me on my ass."

"I can handle 'em."

There was a gentle melancholy to her voice. He studied her face for a trace, a reflection of hatred for what he'd done to her. There was nothing obvious behind her words. He detected no deep resentment festering beneath her politeness.

"It's been a long time," he suggested.

He found it difficult to make small talk when confronted by a deep trough of ancient guilt. She seemed to ignore his discomfort. A faint smile crossed her silver colored lips, revealing less than perfect teeth:

"Too long. I lost my husband and my kids. But that's just how it goes. Life sucks. But I'm getting by."

Despite the words, the tenor of her voice was even, as if depression and decay were commonplace in her life, as if tragedy was something she readily accepted.

"I'm sorry."

He wondered whether he was apologizing for his conduct three decades ago or for her present circumstance.

"Thanks."

"I've never been married myself," he admitted.

"I know."

"How's that?"

"I keep up on what the class is doing."

"Oh."

"Not on everything. It's not like high school was some wonderful experience for me that I want to relive."

The moment became strained. He wanted to walk away, to leave her before she launched into the reasons why, including his own behavior, school had been less than memorable for her.

"Want to dance?" she asked.

Her question caught him unaware. The brimming confidence that defined his stature with his former classmates vanished beneath her inquiry.

"Sure."

They danced hard and fast to old songs. From the first go, he knew she was a good dancer. He'd never asked her to dance in school. It dawned on him that he hadn't even asked her to dance on this occasion.

Jackson Browne's *Running on Empty* erupted from the loudspeakers. They twirled and slid across the hardwood in a panicked search for lost youth. His eyes never left her. It was exciting, exhilarating for him to consider that a terrible dark secret existed between them that she had either completely completely forgiven or completely forgotten.

Jimmy Mancetti's arms slid around her waist as the first notes of *Bell Bottom Blues* echoed off the peeling paint of the hall. He pulled her tight against his body

130

and felt her breasts flatten against his chest. His shirt was damp with perspiration. His pelvis fit snugly against her thigh. He knew she'd soon detect the migration of his blood. An intoxicating odor of Opium perfume and liquor emanated from her as they wove a determined course through the other couples on the floor.

When the lights came on at the end of the evening, Jimmy Mancetti and Gloria Tucker were nowhere in sight.

"God you're beautiful," Mancetti reflected aloud as he watched her walk naked across her bedroom. Gloria's trailer home sat in a desolate hollow deep within the flood plain of the Rice River. She'd managed to save enough money waitressing to buy five acres of untillable bottomland that no one else wanted. Her dad helped her buy a beat up old unit that had seen better days. Gloria lived alone in her trailer along the placid waters of the stream, her kids having been placed with her mother-in-law when Gloria could no longer deal with them or her grief.

Taken in parts, her nude body was striking, though not perfect. Her breasts were symmetrical but sagged under the weight of life, leaving her tawny nipples downcast but excited. Her legs were deeply tanned, tending to thicken near her thighs. Her stomach was flat, accented by nearly invisible stretch marks. The faint scars criss-crossed her belly just above her pelvis. Her pubic hair was auburn and untrimmed. Gloria's thighs did not touch as she moved towards him. The gap between her legs left a suggestion that the most intimate recesses of her body were open and accessible.

As he watched Gloria walk, her arms modestly placed across her chest, Mancetti realized he was messed up. He'd downed eight or nine rum and cokes and smoked a couple of joints with Beth out in the parking lot before he and Gloria hooked up. He contemplated that his performance would likely be less than stellar. But then, what did it matter? He was only going to screw Gloria DeSmedt.

She joined him in her bed. He was already naked. A sultry wind blew in from an open window. He reached for his khakis hanging from one of the bedposts. The finish of the brass post was scratched and dented. His hand dug deep into a pocket, searching urgently for his wallet.

"You won't need that," she whispered. "I'm fixed," she explained, her voice soft and understanding.

Pressure built within him like water behind a dam. He removed his hand from his trousers. Her wiry hair brushed against the skin of his face as he pulled her body onto his. Gloria's smell, the deep scent of a woman in excitement, mingled with the artificial sweetness of her cologne. He tried to hold back, to insure that it would be perfect for her. He wanted to make up for what he'd done to her when she was someone else. He was so screwed up on booze and pot, he couldn't tell when she climaxed; though he had little doubt that she did.

He tried to call her several times after that. All he ever got was her answering machine. The messages he left were never returned.

They hadn't fucked. They'd made love. He couldn't get her out of his mind. It shocked him to find out how soft and sentimental he'd become. There was no reason for him to remember Gloria any differently than the dozens of other women he'd slept with. It troubled him deeply that his "live and let live" attitude, his tried and true protection against emotional entanglement, couldn't withstand thirty years of remorse and one evening of sex.

A few months passed. Someone told him Gloria Tucker had sold her place on the River and moved to the Twin Cities. He tried looking her up when he was down in Minneapolis for business. He had no luck finding her.

It took nearly a year for the symptoms to begin. At first, he ignored them, thinking he had a touch of the flu. When he couldn't shake the fatigue, when he couldn't keep his dinner down, when the sarcomas appeared, Jimmy finally saw a doctor.

THE ICE CREAM PARLOR

She sat near the window, where clear glass surveyed the Plaza in Old Santa Fe. Ebony hair, newly refreshed, as if she had just stepped out of the shower and toweled the fibers dry, was pulled tight and held by a silver and turquoise comb just above the base of her neck. She was a tall woman. A pair of fatigued Lees covered her long legs. A crisp linen shirt, a man's shirt, cloaked her upper body, leaving much to the imagination. Cheap Nike sandals prevented her bare feet from touching the freshly polished white and black linoleum squares of the ice cream parlor floor.

I waited in the back of the restaurant for my sundae. There were dozens of other tourists like me at the counter standing patiently in the late-afternoon light. Some of the women were, in strictly Vogue or Cosmopolitan Magazine terms, better looking than she was. Still, I could not take my eyes off her. I tried not to stare, applying all of the visual techniques I'd learned from nights spent in saloons looking at beautiful women through pretense and oblique glances.

Her legs were crossed seductively. She sat at a counter near a big bay window in the front, writing something on the top page of a stack of loose notebook paper. The afternoon sun cast a friendly glow across her wrists, hands, and fingers, gently delineating those places where her tanned skin was exposed. A clean, straight jaw, high cheekbones and wide, dark eyes defined her face. Fine wisps of black hair, accented by a few random touches of gray, framed the edges of her neck.

Intimate profiles, evidence of her gender, became visible each time she shifted her weight and turned on her stool. The faint impressions of her chest strained the starched cotton of the fabric each time she raised her pen to her lips. She wore no makeup. Her lips were soft, dry, and slight.

Though it was early April in New Mexico, the weather was cool. Insignificant snow fell up north at Taos Pueblo. As I looked at her, I thought about the snow. She had the aloof poise of a downhill skier set hard into the faint lines of her forehead.

Despite the coolness of the day, made cooler by the slow westward march of the sun, patrons continued to enter and depart the store as I considered the woman.

I watched her pause and stare absently at the tourists walking across the village square, the details of her profile captured by the smooth glass of the window. She bit the corner of her lip as she contemplated the scene before her.

Two lean men in dusters, authentic Stetsons, spurred cowboy boots, and blue jeans met up on the sidewalk directly outside the ice cream shop. Their faux ranch clothing caught my eye. The woman seemed oblivious to the costumes or the men. She resumed writing.

The manner of her concentration created an uneasy tension in her eyes but revealed nothing about her literary chore:

Dear Jason:

I can't continue on like this. You swore you'd get help. You haven't. You swore there would be no more women. You told me that Friday's fight would be our last, the last time you'd hit me, the last time you'd threaten me, the last time you'd lay a hand upon my face. Again, that's proven to be anything but the truth.

We've been together for five years. Hanna is nearly four. She's seen us at our worst. When she came into out lives, I think it killed what had been the best between us. I won't let her be raised in an abusive, broken home. I won't let her hear the words or see the anger anymore.

Your stuff is at Pat's house. He said you can store it there as long as you want. I kept a few things that you might want but, you know what? I don't think you deserve them the way you've broken me.

I had Emilio change the locks on the apartment. My phone number is unlisted. We can work out visitation at the Visitation Center during the next week or so. I'll call you at Pat's. I don't want you to see Hanna outside of that until you can prove to me that you're remaining sober and that she'll be safe.

Jason, you're almost thirty-five. It's time you realize you can't bully the world, or me for that matter, into giving you what you think you need. I regret that we ever met. I regret that you ever came into my life; the single exception to that being Hanna's conception. Beyond that, you gave me nothing of significance or value.

I wish I could end this note "Love, Jenny" but you beat that emotion to death. I'm leaving before the rest of my heart suffers the same fate.

Jen

"Your sundae's ready," a pony-tailed teenager called out to me across the room.

I stood up. The woman continued to write, engaged in a private dialogue with paper and pen:

Grocery List
Bread
Six Pack of Falstaff
Dell Shampoo
I Can't Believe It's Not Butter (tub style)
Quart 1% Milk
Dove face soap
Deodorant
Tampax
Newspaper

"That'll be three-fifty-seven," the cashier said. I reached into my pocket and handed him a five. Youthful fingers grasped the money from behind the counter.

"Thanks," I mumbled as the clerk handed me the change. I shoved the bill and the uncounted loose coins deep into the front pocket of my slacks. The ice cream in the paper cup was cold against the bare skin of my palm. As I walked towards the tall woman, she didn't notice my presence or my less-than-subtle attempt to view her work:

Another Day in Santa Fe
By Jennifer Dement

She spent most of her free time near the Plaza. She liked it there. The tourists were akin to strange, wonderful animals in a zoo. Here, a German couple laughed in their coarse, harsh language. There, a Negro family from Detroit, black skins shining naturally in the sun, quietly studied the white light of the high desert.

Then there were the married men who watched her when they thought she wasn't paying attention. She considered them to be immature, unfaithful. Not that she minded the looks. She was not that pure.

Warm fudge and cold ice cream coated my throat in a heavy paste. I stopped eating as I approached her, hopeful that she'd notice me and perhaps grace me with a smile. She remained dedicated to her writing:

Recipe for Duck
1 field-dressed mallard (3-5 lbs.)
2 whole oranges
1 whole onion
1 stalk celery
1 can cream of celery soup

Wash duck. Peel oranges and onion. Wash celery. Dice celery, onions, and oranges. Stuff duck with mixture of same. Place mallard in ceramic roasting pan on a steel rack so that duck is out of its juice. Place remaining mixture around duck in pan. Cover duck and mixture with soup. Bake at 350 degrees for 2 hours. Serve with rice.

I cast a longing glance at the woman's handsome profile as I opened the door and walked out into the brisk mountain air, certain that more than a thin pane of glass separated our lives.

QUANTICO

I keep my eyes focused to the front. I do not glance right or left to see if the Gaskin twins are wearing their perpetual, goofy expressions on their mirror-image faces. The sun beats down on my platoon. We stand at rigid attention on the blacktopped surface of the parade deck. We remain motionless in the thick humidity of the late August air. Silence resonates from the deep green of the Virginia wood surrounding us.

For an hour, no one moves. No one speaks. Perspiration forms under my helmet liner. The liner is painted silver to identify me as an officer candidate, a "chrome dome". Beads of sweat escape from the webbing of the liner and slide down my nose. The drops tickle. Moisture forms under my arms, staining the starched perfection of my fatigue shirt. I stare at nothing. I try to remain as still as a statue.

Candidate Thomas stands right in front of me. He is alone. Sergeant Rice, our drill instructor, stands directly behind Thomas. The soldier faces us, his eyes straight ahead. His green soft cover, his fatigue cap, is pulled down tight on his enormous, round head. Folds of skin flow down the back of his neck like living steps. Thomas is a big man. He claims to play nose tackle for some college back in his home state of West Virginia. He looks like he could do the job. As he stands, he thrusts his chest out in defiance, seemingly daring all comers. Tiny ears peak out from beneath the stiff fabric of his cap. The ears, small and damaged, do not fit the man's body.

Thomas remains front and center. He is dressed from head to toe in green. From talking to him, I know he's accustomed to doing as he pleases. Standing on the hot pavement, his facial skin is slowly turning brilliant pink under the intensity of the Confederate sun.

Sergeant Rice is slender and of average height. He stands a full head shorter than Thomas does. The sergeant is black. Though Rice's African features are concealed within the shadow cast by the football player, I can see that a poisoned expression occupies Rice's face. The noncommissioned officer's glare bores a hole right through Thomas.

There is movement. Rice begins to circle the candidate. Slowly, deliberately, the drill instructor eyes his charge from starched cap to polished boots. The Sergeant's inspection of the man is agonizing to watch.

"Thomas, are you in uniform?"

Rice's voice booms across the parade ground. There is bitter disrespect in his tone. His words contain the same sort of disgust that has pushed us through three weeks of basic training.

"Yes Platoon Sergeant," Thomas responds weakly, his skin quivering in nervous fear. Despite the terror, Thomas' eyes remain forward.

"Does that include your undershirt, Candidate?

"Yes, Platoon Sergeant."

"Does that include your stockings, Candidate?"

"Yes, Platoon Sergeant."

"Does that include your BVDs, Candidate?"

"BVDs, Platoon Sergeant?" the big man answers in a waning voice.

A faint smile crosses the drill instructor's face. The brim of the sergeant's campaign hat shades the smaller man's eyes from the direct light of the sun but I can see that his mouth is open, revealing small white teeth. As he smiles, the pink of Rice's tongue is exposed, the color in marked contrast to the man's dark skin.

"Your goddamned underwear, Thomas. Do you have your USMC-approved, government-issued, taxpayer-financed, mother-fucking underwear on?"

Thomas's breathing grows labored. Fiery crimson spreads across his already sunburned cheeks. For the first time, his eyes drop to the ground.

"No, Platoon Sergeant," Thomas replies in a hesitant voice.

"Be so kind, Candidate, as to tell us all why you are so superior, so special, that you, and you alone, do not see fit to wear the underpants that the United States Marine Corps issued to you for your stay here at Camp Upshire."

There is no answer. Thomas's eyes are clouded. His body rocks back and forth as if he is trying to will himself back to the mountains of West Virginia.

"Thomas, are you buck-assed naked underneath your fatigues? Is this some sort of mountain-folk thing? Like sleeping with your sister?" the sergeant goads. "That is something you folks do, way back in the hills, isn't it Candidate, sleep with your sister?"

"No, Platoon Sergeant."

There is a long, agonizing pause in the conversation.

"What the hell are you wearing under your trousers, Candidate Thomas?"

A tear escapes the big man's left eye. Gravity pulls on the moisture, causing it to slide slowly down the soldier's face. The tear makes a path through the thin dust covering Thomas' cheek. The resulting track reminds me of the slime trail left behind by a slug negotiating a hot sidewalk.

"My girlfriend sent me somethin' to wear," the beaten man chokes.

Rice's face flashes. I know the look, the same look Rice gave me when he found my footlocker out of order and tossed all of my belongings out, through the open door of my Quonset hut. All my underwear, socks, and personal items were strewn up and down the road, trampled by passing soldiers into the black dirt of Virginia. I sense that Thomas is about to suffer something far worse than a few dirty socks.

"Candidate, kindly undress and show your platoon what it is that your girlfriend sent you."

Rice is in the big man's space as he speaks. He stares into the largeness of his charge.

That old mountain boy will kill him, I think. *Thomas 'll grab the mean old bastard with his bare hands and strangle Rice where he stands,* I theorize.

But the West Virginian is beaten. He brings no violence upon his tormentor. Slowly, with tears flowing freely, Thomas unlatches the buckle of his belt. Shiny brass catches the power of the sun and flashes light across the first rank of our platoon. Thick lineman's fingers struggle with buttons. One by one, the stubborn fasteners protecting Thomas' modesty pop free. Thomas hides his face as he labors to release himself from his military trousers.

"Pull 'em all the way down so that these boys can see what it is you feel compelled to wear under the uniform of the United States Marine Corps, Candidate Thomas."

A labored sigh escapes the soldier as he pushes the harsh fabric of the pants down his thickly muscled thighs. I cannot help but stare. I feel the beginnings of a grin swell across my face.

Rice's eyes are riveted on the progress of the trousers.

Cautiously, I chance a look around. The rest of my platoon has the same unconscious smirk etched upon its collective face as I do.

Candidate Thomas stands before us, six-foot-three, two hundred and forty-seven pounds of West Virginia football prowess. He stands there, his pants around his ankles, his eyes lowered to the ground, his pale white legs in stark contrast to the vivid canary yellow of the bikini briefs he is wearing; briefs which do not begin to conceal the suggestion of his manhood.

ISLANDS

Jacob Ellefson looked across Katherine Lake and considered his situation. Ellefson believed that his location was concealed by the reeds and by the irregular brush demarcating the island's shoreline. He thought that he'd covered his tracks. The cabin's aluminum rowboat and three-horsepower outboard motor remained undisturbed back at the boat landing, solidifying the illusion that no one could have crossed the lake and taken refuge on the island. There was only one boat on the lake, only one cabin. As he surveyed the picture before him, it seemed perfect.

He hadn't meant to take the girl. All he wanted was some money, a little kiss, maybe a little foolin' around before he hit the road. It was just plain bad luck she was young and good-looking.

Sure, he knew what they'd be saying on the news: Jake Ellefson, two-time convicted sex offender raped pretty little Maggie. That's where the newscast stopped in his mind. He never did get the teenager's last name.

It sure seemed easy. In retrospect, he should have paid greater heed to his old urges. Even though he'd gone through plenty of treatment at the Moose Lake Psychopathic Hospital, after being placed there on an indefinite civil commitment once his second prison sentence ran out; and even though he felt damn near normal, cured, so to speak, he should have been able to see it coming.

It was a rinky-dink little convenience store up the Gunflint Trail that he chose to rob. He'd had enough working himself to a lather at Torvinson's Lumber Mill in Tofte. He'd had enough $7.00 an hour laboring jobs that left his body dead tired with little coin in his pocket. He knew he was destined for bigger and better things. He had confidence that he could make a new start, find a lady to settle down with who could tame his nature, maybe have some kids that actually loved him. All he

143

needed was a few thousand bucks so he could disappear.

Isla Mujeres, the island of women. He knew enough Spanish to get by. It wouldn't be that hard to get across the border in South Texas and then make his way to the Yucatan. He'd heard it was beautiful down there; plenty of suntanned young women and brilliant Caribbean sunshine. He deserved a break but didn't see one coming along on its own. Destiny required a little help at times and Jake Ellefson was ready to oblige.

"Can I help you?"

She stood behind the counter in the little grocery and gas place, Donovan's Corner it was called, on a bend in the Gunflint Trail just outside of Grand Marais, Minnesota. The store was open all night. Because it was the off-season, the till wasn't emptied but once a week. There was no rush of fishermen or canoe outfitters going up the trail in late November. The tourists had all headed back to the Twin Cities when the last of the leaves fell off the maples along the bluffs overlooking Lake Superior. Deer season had come and gone. There was scant snow cover. A strange, different sort of early winter had begun to show itself in Northeastern Minnesota over the last few years. Temperatures plummeted into the teens during the night but warmed up to the mid-fifties on most days when the sun was out. Any ice that formed on the local lakes and streams melted from the warmth.

He noticed right away how cute the kid was. She couldn't have been more than fifteen. In the past, before he got better, before he learned how to deal with the insanity of his sexual urges, she was exactly the kind of female that set him off. His two convictions involved girls of about the same age. The difference was that those other girls weren't necessarily virgins before they met Jacob. They certainly weren't left as such when he was done with them.

144

He'd picked up his first victim on Hennepin Avenue in Minneapolis near the Nicollet Mall. That was nearly fifteen years ago. He remembered his first as he studied the clean lines of the clerk's jaw in the convenience store, as he watched the girl's eyes examine his face for a trace of who he was, what he wanted.

Natalie; Natalie Brunstein was his first. A heavy-jawed Jewish girl on the run from domineering parents. He thought she was a hooker when he bought her a drink at one of the taverns along Hennepin. He had forty bucks to spend for the night. Her curly black hair, curved hips, and deep brown eyes made her appear older than the sixteen she turned out to be. When they went back to his room at the old Drake Hotel, a rat-infested hovel of a dump just off the beaten path, she wanted no part of his fondling or fooling around.

Jacob had been patient with Natalie. He made her a drink. A brandy and Coke. He slipped her a few downers on the side. His assault on her was so violent that when he was done with her, blood covered the floor and stained the carpet. The feeling of power, of being in complete command, increased his libido to levels that were uncontrollable. He forced her to do things he'd only seen in magazines. He coveted her legs, her face; the deepest reaches of her body, until he found satisfaction there.

Ellefson made the mistake of untying Natalie's hands so she could use the bathroom. He didn't see the harm since the only window in the lavatory was too small for her to escape from and too high for her to hang out of and scream for help. He felt like a fool when he realized that he'd left all of his toiletry items, his razor, his soap, his toothbrush, and toothpaste by the sink. Natalie made sure all of his belongings, including a pocket vanity mirror, went sailing out the window. It was a one in a million shot that the stuff landed on a cop car.

"I need some Marlboro Lights and a couple of twelve packs of Bud Ice."

He figured the clerk was too young to sell cigs or beer but he'd try. She didn't hesitate. She rang them up.

"And I filled up on pump number 1 outside."

She punched the numbers on the console and added the gas to his bill.

"Anything else?"

It was after 10:00pm. The deep forest surrounding the place was silent and foreboding. There were no other cars on the road. There was no one else around for miles. He had a powerful necessity stored inside him from all the days and nights he'd spent alone since his conditional release from commitment. The compulsion was so strong he thought she might be able to read it on his face, detect it in his eyes. There was no trace of recognition in her expression.

His second victim had been a little older, a little more difficult. He had nearly killed her because she fought so damn hard. He didn't want to. Even though rationality would seem to conclude that killing a rape victim would pretty much eliminate her testimony, the urge, the command inside him didn't initially lean that way.

There'd never been a beautiful woman who cast a second glance at Jacob Ellefson's prematurely balding head, complete with its beady, nondescript eyes, set precariously on top of his unattractively morbid body. If a decent looking woman made eye contact with Jacob Ellefson, it was only by accident. Jacob saw that in women's eyes and it angered him.

It was the same way in high school in Edina, the once-wealthy suburb of Minneapolis where Jacob grew up. His rearing in Edina was a cruel joke, an accident perpetrated upon him by his mother. When he was a newborn, she left Jake on the doorstep of some rich guy she'd had a fling with. His real dad was a truck driver from Des Moines who took no responsibility for Jacob's existence even though the kid was conceived in the sleeper cab of the guy's truck. The rich paramour, a dentist, turned out to be a widower with two kids of his own. The man also had a heart. He took Jake in, adopted him, and tried to integrate the child into his family.

But Jacob Stranlund being adopted and renamed Jacob Ellefson didn't change the genetic cesspool the kid came from. The succession of wives that migrated into the dentist's home did little to leave a positive maternal imprint on the boy. While his adoptive siblings seemed to develop an ability to weather the domestic unrest that came and went with the parade of ex-Mrs. Ellefson's, Jacob never learned how to keep his nose clean.

He got bounced out of Edina West High School when he assaulted a baton twirler at a football game. His expulsion wasn't only because he felt her up against her will. It was more due to the fact that he knocked her over the head with a wrench trying to gain her acquiescence.

Gigi Schelhause was his second one. He'd done his three years for the attack on Natalie, gone through AA, maintained sobriety for a year and a half, and was dating a nice lady from St. Paul who worked as a legal secretary, Paula Byrnes, before he met Gigi.

He was working hard with Paula on the sex thing, on trying to have a normal relationship. But no matter how creative, no matter how satisfying their trysts were, it wasn't the same. There was no power, no authority yielded to him in their couplings. He achieved climax but it was a flat, dismal shadow of what he felt when he'd taken Natalie without her permission.

He met Gigi at the law firm where Paula worked. No one there knew his past. He'd had his name changed through the courts and reported the change to the Bureau of Criminal Apprehension so he wouldn't get his probation jerked. It was at a firm Christmas Party that he and Gigi, barely eighteen-years-old and working as a part-time receptionist at Olson and Kraft, first met.

He was certain, as he always was of such things, that the meeting had little impact on her. But their chance introduction had a significant impact upon Jacob. She was a striking young woman, with straight blond hair, a cute smile and a modest demeanor. Though she paid little attention to him at the party, their one brief encounter was enough to captivate Jake in the most delirious of ways. He became obsessed with her, following her whenever he could, watching her every move, even going so far as to catalog her daily activities at Normandale Community College where she was a freshman.

The agony, the yearning, the pressure built and built over the weeks. His less-than celebratory couplings with Paula dwindled away to nothing. His visits to her place, his phone calls to her, dried up under the withering comparison of the thirty-two-year-old secretary to new fruit on the vine.

It was easy to gain access to Gigi's apartment building in Inver Grove Heights. The security door often remained ajar for a few seconds after someone entered. He simply waited until a tenant went in, made sure the person was gone, and then walked into the place without a fuss. It was Sunday evening. He'd watched Gigi enough to know that it was laundry night. He entered the 2nd floor laundry room, a slender Buck knife unsheathed and concealed within the sleeve of his jean jacket, and selected a dark corner in which to wait. It wasn't long before she padded across the linoleum, a laundry basket under one arm, to check a load in the dryer. Gigi had no opportunity to defend herself, no chance to scream as he held the knife to her throat and dragged her back to her room.

She was better than Natalie. She was a strong, healthy, athletic young girl. He was an out of shape thirty-year-old with limited strength but much determination. He taped her mouth with silver duct tape and tried to force the loose cotton pajama bottoms off her legs. She fought him. She struck at his eyes with her fists and dug her fingernails deep into the skin of his jowls. He wore a ski mask but his eyes clearly reflected desire. His need to conquer her increased exponentially with the vigor of her defense.

A neighbor's knock on the door the next morning spoiled everything. Jacob had no desire to kill the girl; though the brutal beating he gave Gigi Schelhaus nearly accomplished her death. Once the neighbor ceased pounding on the door, advising in a loud voice that she was calling the Inver Grove Heights Police, Ellefson left. He believed he would not be caught. Unfortunately for Jacob, he left his wallet on the end table next to his victim's bed.

Eight years of being sexually assaulted in the showers at Oak Park Heights Maximum Security Correctional Facility in Stillwater, Minnesota taught Jacob Ellefson two things. One. He was definitely not a homosexual; he didn't enjoy being raped by other men. And two, he was never going to go to prison again.

"I want whatever you got in the till."
"Excuse me?"
"You heard me." Give me all the money you got in that there cash register."

With speed that defied his bulk, Ellefson was behind the counter and had a firm hold of the cashier. As his fingers tightened across the back of her upper arm, old desires began to surface. He fought them. God, how he fought them. He tried to force them down, back into the pit of sin and perdition that created them. He couldn't resist their strength. The girl's fragrance, the smell of youth mixed with a touch of fear, was an elixir that he couldn't refuse.

Thoughts bounced within his head. Taking her, doing her, killing her. She hadn't done anything to him. She was someone's daughter. Some boy in town likely loved her.

Don't do this, his mind told him. *Don't do what you want to do.*

She was so small. Her meager struggles against his grip were without merit. He was able to hold her hostage with his dominant left hand and remove the money from the till with his right. She began to cry. He wondered why she didn't scream out. He didn't have a free hand to cover her mouth at that point. He issued a hasty warning:

"I've got a gun in my pocket. You scream, I'll shoot you here and leave you to bleed to death on the floor."

The words hissed over his yellow teeth like steam out of a boiler. He was lying. He didn't have a gun. He couldn't legally buy a gun because he was a felon. Up until he planned to rob the place, he'd stayed away from anything that would send him back to prison. Now that caution no longer mattered, he wished he'd brought a gun.

Ellefson shoved bills deep into the pockets of his Wranglers. The girl began to resist as he forced her out of the store. It was too late. He was free to clamp one hand over her mouth and apply the entire extent of his strength to control her. Though he was firm in his determination to get her into his vehicle, he moderated his grasp. He didn't want her dead before he took her. Making love to a dead girl would be grotesque. She had to be alive to struggle, to compel the juices within him to soar. It had been a long time since he'd been with a woman. He had a lot of catching up to do.

"Stop trying to bite me or I'll kill you right here."

He slapped the girl across the face and shoved her into the cab of his truck. The Dodge half-ton was perfect for the job. It had electric locks and the lock on the passenger side was busted. It could only be opened from the outside. He pushed the crying, hysterical girl across the bench seat, across the dust and ripped vinyl, and climbed in.

150

The truck roared to life as he stomped on the accelerator and spun out on loose gravel. As the vehicle's speed increased, Jake listened to the wailing girl and began to feel that maybe he'd made a mistake. He traced his options over and over in his mind as the rusty blue pickup bounded east on the Trail. Reaching past the distraught girl, he dug deep into the glove box and found a Kleenex.

"Here."

Nervously, she extended her tiny hand and took the tissue.

"What's your name?"

She stopped dabbing at her tears and began to sob.

"Stop that shit or I'll blow your brains out right here, right now. There's nothing that crying is gonna help and you ain't getting out of here until I decide what to do."

There was a period of silence as the girl tried to suppress her weeping.

"That's better. Tell me what your name is."

"Maggie. Margaret."

Her voice was small; becoming smaller as each letter escaped her lips.

Headlights appeared below the crest of a hill. A forest service road sign loomed on the right. Ellefson turned without signaling. Margaret burst into tears. Somewhere in the wild hills above Lake Superior, he found a secluded place to have her.

He was surprised at how well she took it and how little the world seemed to care that a fifteen-year-old girl had lost her innocence. A small murmur of surprise escaped from Margaret when he pulled himself off her. A tiny gasp of air, no more than a sigh, left her mouth, followed by a brief fluttering of her eyelids were her only reaction to his assault. It eased Jacob's guilt to know that Maggie's end would come swift. He taped her up tight with duct tape and placed her unconscious body in the topper of his pickup. He nestled the girl in between pieces of his gear on an old mattress he sometimes slept on when times were hard.

No one would ever know that he'd raped and killed the girl. Hell, it would likely be years before they ever found her body. He knew how to get rid of things, how to bury things deep where no one could find them. If anyone ever found her body, there'd be pitifully little left to identify.

He lit a cigarette and popped a can of Bud Ice as the truck bounced noisily over gravel, pondering how and when he would do it. Jacob had read the Bible cover to cover during his prison stays. He could pull a relevant verse or two out of his ass. She deserved at least some scripture before he put her to rest. With a name like Margaret, she was probably Catholic. He didn't know much about Catholics. He'd been a Baptist once. The son of a Baptist dentist. Or maybe he was the son of a Catholic trucker. Or a Protestant motherfucker.

He downed another beer, rolled down the window and tossed the aluminum can out into the night. The front wheels of the pickup struck a pothole. The jolt launched the Grumman aluminum canoe strapped to the vehicle's topper into the air.

Thud.

The watercraft resumed its perch on the wooden boat carriers above the truck's cab.

Things went pretty well for a time. He figured he'd use the back roads until he got to Two Harbors. That was the problem with robbing a place up off the North Shore. There weren't many ways to leave. You either had to take a chance on the main road, Highway 61 running from Duluth to Thunder Bay, Ontario, or you had to sneak around on the gravel roads behind the hills until you could find another way to get to Duluth. Looking at the map, he chose to stay out of sight, back behind the bluffs, weaving a less obvious path.

Then the damn Dodge started acting up. Somewhere near the headwaters of the Cloquet River, a thin black stream that made its way south for more than fifty miles before finally joining the St. Louis River just above the City of Cloquet, the truck began to die.

He had little choice. He couldn't keep driving around in the woods with a brutalized teenager in his truck until the vehicle totally quit. The Dodge couldn't be found on the road. If a Lake County Deputy, the only law around, came upon the vehicle, the cop would run the plates. They'd come back to "Jacob Elstrom", his new name, a name he never used when talking things over in his head. That would keep the police at bay for a short while but it wouldn't be long before they put two and two together. An ex-rapist leaves his job a week before his truck is found abandoned in Lake County. A check with the BCA. His old name, his old past gets dredged up. They think: "Hmmmm. Who could have possibly abducted a teenage girl from the Gunflint Trail? Could it be Mr. Ellefson?"

The Dodge staggered. It was obvious that a head gasket was about to go. Ellefson searched for a place to leave the truck. He turned off the main road and followed a brutal logging trail for a short while until the truck's high beams illuminated water. A beaver pond had flooded the roadway precluding further progress.

Ellefson walked gingerly atop the beaver dam, prodding the bottom of the pond with a piece of broken aspen. There were places in front of the dam where the water reached twenty feet in depth. He was a lucky man.

Before he made the truck vanish, Jacob backed the vehicle up to the edge of the bulrushes surrounding Katherine Lake. Climbing out of the heated cab, familiar sounds greeted his ears. The noise was carried to him on a chilly gale from somewhere nearby.

"Horses," he murmured. "Clydesdales, if I recollect."

The sawyer had been in the area once before, with a couple of his buddies from the mill, to fish walleye in early summer. He remembered making a wrong turn past the lake and ending up in a Finnish dairy farmer's yard. Ellefson surmised that the Finlander's cabin, occupying the middle of a small paddock cut into the aspen and birch forest, was no more than a half-mile to the east of Katherine Lake.

As he ambled towards the back of his truck, the rapist tried to recall the details of the farm. The intimate particulars of the homestead were lost to him. He could only remember that there had been horses, big draft horses, a couple of little kids, and a wife of some sort, the physical details of which he couldn't retrieve.

"It'd be damn useful to know such things," Jacob lamented. "Too bad I can't remember shit."

Maggie-with-no-last-name wasn't heavy. Jacob lifted the unconscious form of the teenager out of the topper and placed her limp body gently into the canoe. Bands of tape bound the girl's arms and legs. Blond hair fell across her slender face, obscuring her narrow feminine features from view as he worked at a quick pace under the illumination of the Dodge's headlamps.

He stuffed his sleeping bag, a huge Duluth Pack full of provisions and clothing, a couple of small duffel bags, a Coleman stove, a propane lantern, and a large plastic cooler around the prostrate body of the girl in the middle of the canoe.

The top of the Dodge's passenger cab and topper settled quickly beneath the surface of the beaver pond. Ellefson walked the short path back to the boat landing. Heavy snow began to fall. He watched with satisfaction as the tire ruts left by his truck began to fill up with soft, thick flakes.

"First good luck I've had in months," he mused as he walked past a sign that read:

PRIVATE LAKE. NO PUBLIC ACCESS.

154

"Once I'm warmed up and I've taken care of the girl, I'll pay the Finlander a visit. Seems to me he had a truck or two parked behind the house. Likely I'll find me some keys left right where they oughta be, in the ignition."

Dark water stretched out before the canoe as Jacob paddled with easy, confident strokes learned over years of Boy Scout campouts at the behest of the dentist. His eyes became accustomed to the lack of light and the stark deficiency of stars and moon. Despite the darkness, the rapist was able to follow a well-worn channel through thick reeds until the bow of his canoe broke free of vegetation and hit open water.

Small waves rolled under the heavily laden craft. A slight draught, blowing snow in from the Arctic, churned the brackish waters of the shallow lake into a chop. Despite the weight of the canoe's cargo, the Grumman sliced through the crests with ease.

Halfway across the open water, the girl began to come to. Her captor steadied his course and pushed with renewed vigor towards the one and only island on the lake. Jacob Ellefson couldn't see his victim's face. He didn't know her eyes were open to the night.

The cabin was locked. Ellefson broke a window on the side of the building facing away from the boat launch. He broke the window closest to a sign reading:

NO TRESPASSING-PRIVATE PROPERTY.

Ellefson entered the structure. The bright beam of his halogen pocket flashlight offered a narrow perspective. It was cold inside the cottage. The furniture, old overstuffed chairs and a sleeper-couch, were covered with sheets for the winter season. It was clear that the owners, likely occasional visitors from the Twin Cities, would not be back until summer.

A brisk wind greeted the man as he reached over the gunwale of the canoe and lifted the girl in his arms. She was shivering, and, to his way of reckoning, still passed out from her ordeal. He lumbered through the quickly accumulating snow. His feet sent flakes aloft with each stride. Ellefson re-entered the cabin, placed Maggie on the couch, and trudged back outside.

Ellefson's propane lantern, a cheaper version of a traditional Coleman double mantle, hissed quietly in the still air of the frigid room. There was one main chamber to the place; a single room contained the living, eating, and sleeping quarters. A small sleeping porch, its screens covered with plywood sheets stained light brown to match the varnished pine logs of the cabin walls, stretched across the front of the building. Each of the plywood panels was padlocked, preventing entry to the porch from the outside.

A small propane space heater was mounted to a wall of the porch. An LP gas tank was located outside. Ellefson's inspection told him the container was full of gas, likely left that way so as to be ready for opening fishing in May. Bending in front of the wall stove, the logger opened a valve and lit a match. A steady wave of heat began to warm the air.

He re-situated the girl on the sagging mattress of a rollaway bed in the porch. She had nowhere to run, nowhere to hide, even if she was able to extract herself from the tape wrapped dangerously tight around her wrists, mouth, and ankles. Ellefson knew that her existence was measured in rapidly passing time; measured in hours, not days.

Time. He sat in the thick cold of the main room. A small fire burned in a brick fireplace. No other source of heat was available in the cabin proper. Ellefson watched flames reflect off stained log walls. He relished the taste of ice-cold beer. Though he was on his way to becoming drunk, his intent was clear. In the past, his will had failed him, failed to allow him to do the thing that separated the men from the boys. Ellefson hoped that alcohol would give him the courage, or at least, abate the fear, so that he could do what needed to be done.

"Can't afford to leave her behind," he told himself aloud, his diction dancing artfully around his tendency to slur his words when drunk.

"I'm not going back to fuckin' prison."

A gust blew hard outside.

"What the hell."

His voice was loud. The revelation hit him in mid-thought, causing him to be upset with his stupidity, his lack of foresight.

"Why didn't I just leave her in the goddamned truck? It'd be months before anyone found her. By then, I'd be on Isla, long gone from this shithole."

But then, as quickly as the suggestion appeared, self-doubt and reality clouded the idea:

"That wouldn't work. They'd trace it to me. Then they'd know who done it. Better this way, that she dies out here, slips beneath the water, and disappears."

There was a stirring in the other room. Jacob struggled to rise. The yellow glow cast by the gas lantern cloaked the porch in paltry light. Ellefson saw that the girl had managed to spin around in bed. She was sitting upright. The chord secured to her neck was taut. Ellefson had tied the far end of the rope to an iron ring bolted to an interior wall. The line prevented Maggie from leaving the bed.

"So you're awake. I bet you're hungry after our little excursion. You sit tight, I'll get you something."

Large drops of moisture formed in the girl's eyes. Muffled sounds rose from her throat, but died before becoming words.

"Behave yourself, you hear? You fuck around with me when I take this here tape off, you try to scream, and I'll just tape you back up and let you starve. Understand?"

Her eyes stared wildly past the man, seemingly seeking, looking for salvation. More tears appeared and rolled down the juvenile contours of her face.

"Nod if you understand. You hear me? Screw with me and it'll be a long time, if ever, before you get somethin' to eat."

Maggie nodded slightly. Water cascaded from her eyes like rain. Deep sobs shook her torso as she followed her captor's hands. He unsheathed his hunting knife. Uncontrollable shivering caused the rope to constrict around the adolescent's neck, compromising her ability to breathe. A wave of fear disrupted her gaze as she focused on the path of the blade arcing towards her jugular.

"There. That wasn't so bad, was it?"

Ellefson pulled the cleanly severed tape away from her unblemished skin with a steady motion. He raised a can of Mountain Dew to her lips. She drank greedily of the sweet potion, pausing only when the gas bubbles began to rise up inside her stomach. His thick, ugly fingers held a chocolate chip granola bar to her clean white teeth; teeth straightened and beautified by countless trips to the orthodontist.

"I'm Jacob. You may not want to know that, given where we are and what's gone on. But you've got a right to know."

Her eyes stared down at the bare pine planks of the floor. She chewed the grainy mixture slowly, without relish, clearly eating only to satisfy the most basic of instincts. It took an inordinate amount of time for the girl to swallow.

"Don't feel like talking, eh? I can appreciate that."

His scarred hands made quick work of the remaining tape.

In the silence that followed, as he took his time and assailed her innocence once again, smothering her resistance beneath the weight of his body, the rapist believed Maggie recognized that the precarious existence

158

remaining her was dependent upon Jacob Ellefson's generosity. He was glad she was such a smart girl, such a perceptive learner.

When it was over, Jake made sure that she was bound and that the knife, which he'd carelessly left next to her on the bed, was sheathed and on his belt. As he lay beneath a tattered quilt on the couch in front of the sparse fire, his eyes grew heavy. The beer's glow had expired. Though the liquor failed to amass the courage he needed to end the girl's life, there was no way around it. Tomorrow he would have to kill her.

It'd be done quickly so as to avoid causing her undue suffering. He'd weigh her down and drop her over the side of the Grumman. There was one deep hole, a little less than fifteen feet deep, in the lake. That would be where she'd have to rest.

Dawn came slowly from the east. The cabin was ice cold. Ellefson was hung over and ornery when the first rays of the sun touched his forehead, waking him from a fitful sleep. The logger swung his bulky legs over the edge of the couch. He pulled on his leather hunting boots one boot at a time. There were no embers left in the fireplace.

"Strange," Ellefson mumbled beneath his breath, "the heater on the porch should have kept this place warmer."

He felt like a cigarette. The girl could wait. She wasn't going anywhere. The man pulled out a butt and clamped it between his teeth. Slowly, as if a daze, Jacob reached into the upper left pocket of his work shirt, the fabric worn and green, and searched for a light.

"Where'd I put those damn matches?"

Ellefson stood up and checked all of his pockets. There were no matches to be found. He tucked the cigarette back into the pack.

"It'll keep. Must be a sign that it's time. Stop delaying, making excuses. You want to get away clean, to make it to Isla and all them pretty women. It's a thing you gotta do and do now."

Though his dialogue with himself was impassioned, he kept his voice low. Ellefson didn't want to excite Maggie or give her any indication of what was coming. He wasn't in the mood for even the briefest of struggles. He was cold, tired, and in the mood to see if one of the Finlander's vehicles would start.

Jacob found the girl huddled in a ball under the covers of the bed, her small form curled up tightly against the cold.

"Must have quit working in the night," Jacob said, glancing in the general direction of the wall heater. It was obvious no heat was coming from the unit.

Sounds from outside interrupted the man's thought process. He was just about to pull the girl out from beneath the covers when the familiar displacement of oars against water captured his undivided attention.

Standing to one side of the big picture window facing the landing, Jacob considered the approach of a fishing boat. The craft's progress was agile against the weather. The snow had stopped. Only a few inches had fallen; not nearly enough to conceal the tire tracks of the Dodge.

"Shit."

The rapist inventoried the confines of the room for a weapon. There were no firearms. His knife would be useless against two people. But on the mantle above the fireplace, a small box caught his eye:

"USCG Approved Flare gun. 4 Count Flares".

The criminal opened the box, removed a cheap plastic handled device from the container, broke open the gun, slid a flare into the gun's chamber, and snapped the silver barrel into place.

Click.

There was no sound from the girl on the porch.

The man's eyes leveled. Ellefson followed the path of the fishing boat until the bow of the craft struck the shoreline of the island. He recognized the pram as the boat he'd left behind at the landing: the cabin owner's boat. Sitting on the plank seats were two police officers. Ellefson recognized the brown and tan overcoats covering their uniforms and the brown cowboy hats they held loosely in their gloved hands.

"Lake County Deputies," he muttered.

A female officer stepped heavily onto the ground. Her black leather boots slipped on the fresh snow covering the not yet frozen earth. She steadied herself, put her hat on her head, and looked towards the dwelling with obvious anticipation. She drew a weapon, an automatic. The officer slid the action to the rear, insuring that there was a round in the chamber. Her partner walked gingerly across the seats of the unsteady boat and joined her on the shore.

"You take the front, I'll take the rear," the female officer advised.

Ellefson watched the intruder's split up. The woman walked cautiously towards the cabin and stopped within a few feet of the front door. The rapist watched the woman's partner draw a heavy barreled revolver from its holster and slide between shadows created by a stand of cedar trees.

"Anyone in there? Deb Slater here, Lake County Undersheriff. Come on out now and we'll talk about what's gone on."

Jacob steadied the flare gun in his thick hands. He flattened himself against the smooth log wall of the cabin. The woman approached. The doorknob turned. Ellefson's eyes maintained a vigilant watch on the back door. Timing would be everything. The female cop would have to make her entrance before her partner made it to the back door.

A locked door of solid white pine held together by blackened steel blocked the rear entrance. It would take a strong man considerable time to break the door away from its hinges. Ellefson gauged that he'd have a slight opening to react before he was outnumbered.

Hardware creaked in the cold air. Undersheriff Slater stepped into the dim light of the cottage. In an instant, she felt the cold, unmistakable muzzle of a large caliber weapon measure the bare skin of her neck.

"Tell your partner to come around to the front door. Loosen your grip on that sidearm and ease it to the floor with one finger through the trigger guard."

"You aren't going to get away with this. Do you have the girl? If you do, if she's still alive, we can work things out," the woman advised as she bent to place her handgun on the floor.

"Tell your partner. Ain't none of your business whether the girl's alive or dead. Tell him."

"Jim, he's got me. Got a gun to my neck," the female officer shouted. "He wants you to come around to the front door."

"Tell him to stand by the boat, hands in the air. Tell him to leave his handgun in front of the door, where I can see it," Ellefson directed.

"He won't give up his weapon."

"He will if he doesn't want to see his partner's pretty little head blown to small bits. Tell him, goddamn it."

Jacob studied the woman. Her hair was cut very short. She wore it auburn brown, though there was no telling if the color was natural or dyed. She was solid, not fat, not large, but well put together. He didn't get a good look at her face but he realized, from her profile, that she was pregnant.

The woman hesitated. There was no response from her partner. His footsteps had stopped. Ellefson wasn't sure where the man was.

"I doubt he wants to be responsible for losing his partner and her baby. Tell him now or I'll blow your fuckin' brains to pieces."

The flare gun slid down the woman's spine until it stopped at the center of her back.

"He wants you to come around front, put your weapon on the ground in front of the door, then back up to the boat."

There was only silence.

"OK. I'm doing what he says," a male voice responded.

Ellefson cocked his head to listen to the retreat of the other deputy. The rapist's grip on the flare gun tightened, forcing the barrel deep into the fabric of Debra Slater's storm coat. From the corner of his eye, Jacob watched the male officer trudge slowly across new snow, stop in front of the door, and deposit his revolver in plain view.

"Very good. Now tell him to step back to the boat."

"He wants you to move back to the boat."

The man didn't move. He stood over his weapon, reluctant to leave; uncertain of what lay ahead.

"What is that stupid shit waiting for? What's his last name?"

"LeTour," the woman responded in an emotionless tone.

"Deputy LeTour, do as you're told or your partner and her kid are history."

Jim LeTour, his dark French-Canadian heritage easily distinguishable by virtue of his thick black moustache and black hair, turned and walked towards the water.

"Sit in the front of the boat, facing towards the lake. If you turn your head this way again, the woman dies."

LeTour sat on a bench seat of the boat in awkward compliance and stared blankly at the water. A lazy breeze stirred. The wind formed small whitecaps over the surface of the lake.

"Get on the couch," Ellefson commanded, pushing the woman towards the davenport. Deftly, without

163

breaking stride, the logger scooped up Slater's 9mm as they advanced across the room.

"What are you going to do to me?"

Fear was obvious in the officer's voice. Ellefson tucked the flare gun into the waistband of his jeans and rested his thumb carelessly on the hammer of the automatic before shoving the officer onto the couch.

"Relax. You're what, 30? Not my type. Not my type at all. Roll over."

Placing one knee in the small of the pregnant woman's back, the rapist put all of his weight on his captive. He looped nylon rope around the woman's wrists and brought the knot in tight, rendering her hands useless. In similar fashion, he bound her legs and ankles, saving the last of his duct tape for her mouth, all the while keeping one eye on the male officer out the window.

"That should hold you. Now I'll tell you what's gonna happen, sheriff. I'm gonna go in there, get little missy and haul her little ass out to your partner. Then I'm gonna shoot them both in the back of the head. Don't worry, they'll never feel a thing."

There was a stench, an odor, emanating from the man as he talked. Though his words were spoken in confidence, a slight tremor in his voice betrayed nervousness.

"Then I'll come back in here and do the same to you."

Slater tried to strike out at her captor. Her efforts to rise from the mildewed surface of the couch were futile. Ellefson didn't smile. He didn't relish the fact that the course he'd fallen into, the plan that he had made, required the deaths of two cops. But he couldn't see any way around it. They'd stumbled upon him, way out here, on the island, when by all rights, they shouldn't have. Now they had to be dealt with, in a final and convincing manner, just like Maggie. Poor sweet little Maggie.

The man's eyes stared at the distant outline of the deputy sitting in the rowboat some twenty paces from the cabin's front door. Ellefson didn't want to try and cover the distance between them without a hostage. He wanted his exit from the place to include the girl so that the deputy wouldn't try to move on him. Once LeTour realized Maggie was alive and under the scrutiny of the 9mm, he'd be compliant.

Jacob's pace increased. He held the handgun loosely in his left hand as he crossed the threshold into the porch. The girl was sitting upright, her back towards him, her feet dangling over the far edge of the bed, as he entered the room. He wanted to stop and touch her smooth, adolescent hair, to feel the youthful softness of her skin. There was no time.

"We gotta go," he said in a serious tone of voice as he removed the rope from her neck. A scent of something pungent wafted across his face. The odor danced inside his nostrils.

"What the hell...."

The girl's hands moved desperately. He watched as Margaret's fingers struggled against the duct tape, as she dragged a match across the cover of a matchbook. Propane had settled beneath the rollout bed during the early morning hours after the girl disconnected the copper supply line from the exterior tank. The explosion struck Jacob Ellefson full force and blew the rapist through the far wall of the porch, catapulting his corpse head-over-heels across the ground like an out of control pinwheel.

Jim LeTour sprinted across the front yard, grabbed his weapon, and launched his body through the front door. Making his way to Debra Slater's side, LeTour ripped the tape away from the undersheriff's mouth and hands.

"The girl," Slater gasped. "She's on the porch."

"There's nothing left of the porch."

"I don't care. She was there. Find her."

165

LeTour entered the porch cautiously. Acrid haze singed his lungs and eyes as he searched the remnants of the room for the girl.

"She's not here," the deputy yelled as he came back into the main room.

Fire swept across one wall of the porch. Flames quickly ignited the cedar shakes of the roof. Embers popped and snorted as LeTour helped his pregnant partner out of the conflagration.

"You've got to go back in and look for her," Slater whispered, her voice irritated by smoke. "She's only fifteen."

LeTour studied his boss' eyes:

"I know," he whispered.

Jimmy jogged through the snow, his handgun held at a ninety-degree angle. He approached the body of Jacob Ellefson. There was no need to inspect the corpse. The skin of Ellefson's head had been pulled away from his skull by the force of the blast, rendering the rapist's facial features surreal.

Dodging falling ashes and burning wood, LeTour re-entered the cottage through the opening created by the explosion. The deputy tried to walk across the flooring. Flames and smoke reduced him to shuffling over super-heated pine planks. It was no use. He rose and retreated from the blaze.

"She's over here," Slater called out, her voice high pitched and cloaked with relief.

The female officer was kneeling in the snow, in the middle of a small clump of ground pine twenty feet short of the dead man.

"She's alive," Deb Slater shouted. "Thank God she's alive."

The woman's eyes filled to the brim with tears. The undersheriff touched the delicate skin of the victim's forehead with a gloved hand. The girl's face was blackened by smoke. Maggie's right arm was bent unnaturally away from her body. From her left ankle to her left hip, the girl's blue jeans were reduced to ash, the first layer of her skin was badly burned.

"I used to baby-sit her," Deputy LeTour offered as he approached them.

Crash.

The officer's attention was momentarily diverted as the roof of the cabin collapsed. LeTour turned his head away from the noise and spoke softly into his portable radio, confirming their location, asking for assistance.

"She's Elmer and Martha Emerson's only child," LeTour observed. "How in the hell could something like this happen up here?"

The deputy yanked his arms free of his storm coat and draped the garment over the girl. Debra Slater, her round belly protruding unnaturally, knelt next to the unconscious child. The undersheriff's eyes fixed hopefully upon the distant landing as she waited for the sound of sirens.

REDEMPTION

Dan Logan hunkered down under the eaves of the old house. A thin nylon windbreaker was his only protection against tentacles of cold. Logan stood hidden from view, silently studying the frosted glass of the window in front of him. His form merged with the darkness of the night. Faint light from inside the home outlined a short, middle-aged silhouette of failure.

He had been a Minneapolis policeman for most of his adult life. The bottle had ruined him, ruined him so completely that he had nothing left. No wife, no family, no house. That he was still alive, standing in the piercing cruelty of the cold, was in and of itself a miracle. Or a cruel joke. He pulled the collar of his jacket up to block out the wind as he cast an envious gaze at the home.

The crowbar hidden in his jacket served as a conduit. He felt the metal's frigid sting through the dirty fleece of his sweatshirt. He stood at a moment of decision, a moment that most men come to several times during their lives. He took a deep breath and exhaled. His eyes followed the cloud of his breath as the vapor vanished in the night. It was now or never. He braced a numb foot against the bricks of the building and pulled the wrecking bar from its hiding place. It would be easy. There was no one inside the house.

As he raised the weapon to shatter a windowpane, he saw her as she walked into the room, unaware of the danger. She was a slight girl of eight or nine. Her short blond hair touched the cloth of her cotton nightgown. The crisp fabric rustled as she carried a plate of milk and cookies to the base of the Christmas tree. A perfectly shaped balsam stood over the child. The tree's electric lights were unplugged but its ornaments caught the subtle illumination cast by a stairwell chandelier and reflected silver and gold out onto the fresh snow.

He watched the child, a girl nearly the same age as his own daughter, carefully unfold a note and place it beneath the platter of cookies. He could not read the script but he knew what it said, who it was to. He lowered the crowbar, the rusted iron searing the flesh of his bare hands, and watched as the child retreated towards sleep.

Logan dropped the tool. Thick snow muffled the sound of steel striking frozen ground. No tears fell from his eyes, though they surely fell in the confines of his heart, as Dan Logan faded into solitude.

EASTER IN THE SANGRE DE CRISTOS

Flat snowflakes drift saucer-like through the high desert air. Off to the north, shoulders of mountains rise to touch a platinum sky, their flanks thickly covered by temperate pines.

Augustus de Asis, an Indian boy named after the mission church of the same name, sits motionless on the cold surface of a rough hewn mesquite bench and stares across the central square of Taos Pueblo, his bitterness untouched by the beauty of the place. The adolescent's round eyes, the pupils dominated by unrelenting brown, remain unfocused. All around him, families pass by in reverent silence. It is Easter Vigil, a Holy Day in the faith of Christians. Augustus is a Christian, a Roman Catholic, though the boy does not feel like celebrating the resurrection of a Jewish man two thousand years removed from the experience of the Pueblo.

"Hey," Tommy Benthorn, Augustus' best friend shouts as he approaches with his mother and sister from the parking lot.

The Benthorns don't live on the reservation; Tommy's father died in an industrial accident while working the ski lifts at Angel Fire. By the standards of the world of the Pueblo tribes, the Benthorns are rich. By the standards of the white man's world, they are lower middle class. The wrongful death settlement was enough to break them of the reservation but not enough to make them wealthy.

"Hey," Augustus responds flatly.

"What's wrong, bud?"

"Nothin'."

The Benthorn family continues by. Tommy stops in front of his friend. A look of serious concern flashes across the fifteen-year-old's face.

"That's garbage. I can tell when you're down. What gives?"

"It's none of your business."

Tommy reaches out with his right hand and places it on the other boy's shoulder.

"You're my friend. It's always my business. Is it about Coach Thompson?"

"You wouldn't understand."

Augustus wants to add: "you wouldn't understand because you're not a reservation Indian anymore," but doesn't.

"Suit yourself. Going to church?"

"I think I'll skip it."

"You'll miss Father Baraga's annual Easter Vigil Homily."

The priest's sermon, unchanged since he came from Tucson a decade before to serve Taos Pueblo and three other congregations in Northern New Mexico, is something that few baptized members of the Pueblo miss. Augustus has never, in fact, missed the message since the priest arrived.

"I don't feel like listening to religion tonight."

"I hope you get over whatever's eating you."

"Yeah."

The boys speak to each other in Tiwa, the ancient language of their people. They both know the old ways and can speak in the old tongue.

Dim lantern light illuminates the mission as the Benthorn kid walks away. Shadows shroud the chapel's bell tower as the overcast day departs.

Augustus leans heavily against the adobe wall of his family's pueblo and finds he is unable to overcome his disappointment. Smooth walls of vaguely painted mortar climb behind him in a series of deliberate steps towards a desolate sky as he tries to survey the intricacies of his circumstance.

He'd run as fast as he could, shot the ball as well as his meager talents allowed. It hadn't been enough. His dream of making the Taos High varsity basketball team lay fractured; his delicate vision of success reduced to tiny fragments of possibility irretrievably lost upon the gymnasium floor.

He'd worked so hard for so many years, practicing hour after hour shooting free throws and jump shots under the assaultive heat of mountain summers, his cheap K-Mart ball battered to shreds by the coarse soil of the village courtyard. Even though he knew he was undersized, he thought he had a shot at the team. In hindsight, he should have known better.

To the disenfranchised youth, it seemed likely that Coach Thompson, a stern no-nonsense disciplinarian, knew the boy's reputation, knew his family history; a history of poverty, alcoholism, and shiftless disregard for order. It appeared obvious to Augustus that nothing he did during practice or the two scrimmages he participated in redeemed him in the eyes of the Anglo coach.

That morning, despite the fact it was only a day before Easter, Thompson made them practice. Afterwards, he posted the roster for the varsity squad. The de Asis kid was not on the list.

It had been a sullen walk home. When his mother asked how things had gone, he remained silent. When his Uncle Pat asked whether he had made the team, the kid walked on by without saying a word. By the time Tommy Benthorn approached, Augustus had been sitting on the bench for the better part of four hours, still dressed in his tennis shoes, T-shirt, and gym shorts.

Thirsty, the boy rises and walks with the patient pace of a native person towards the river. A silver thread of stream, the Rio Pueblo de Taos, shimmers beneath the night sky. Flakes of brilliant snow continue to drift to the ground, melting when they contact the earth.

The youth gingerly threads a path down the slippery riverbank and stops near a shallow pool. Upstream from the pond, water cascades noisily over a series of small stones and boulders before settling into quiet. Below the pool, small rapids send the river audibly on its way.

Augustus kneels hesitantly on a cold rock, feeling both defeat and winter in his joints. His brown hands scoop water to his mouth with urgency. Frigid liquid burns his throat as he gulps deeply of the river's offering.

His physical need satisfied, the boy stands upright, extending his frame to its full height in the chilly air. There is movement across the water. Two yellow eyes peer at him from inside a hedge of sagebrush. The wind picks up in gentle fashion, forcing the falling snow into miniature funnel clouds. The creature across the river pauses. It's eyes stare at the Indian youth. The gentle lapping of a canine tongue can be heard over the whistle of the storm.

The Indian studies the coyote for a long time. The wolf returns the boy's gaze until the creature's innate nervousness overwhelms its curiosity. With a single bound, the coyote reverses course and merges with the undergrowth.

"That's an omen."

De Asis recognizes the voice of Father Baraga. The Catholic priest is standing behind the boy.

"What'd ya mean?"

"The wolf. He survives by knowing what to do next."

"What's that got to do with anything?"

The boy realizes his tone is disrespectful. Augustus waits for the priest to chastise him. Instead, the Father simply continues their dialogue:

"I know what happened today."

"How do you know?"

"Do you think anything of importance gets said in this small place that isn't heard by these large ears?"

The Indian considers the tall, thin frame of the cleric. Indeed, the man's ears are disproportionate to the size of his head.

173

"I know what Coach Thompson did. It's not the first time he's made a mistake. But you're only a sophomore. You've got two more chances to make the varsity."

"I'm done with basketball."

"I've seen you play. You've got a wicked jump shot, though your quickness and defense could use refinement."

Snow settles on the priest's hassock. The village beyond the riverbank remains quiet.

"How do you know so much about basketball?" the boy skeptically asks the white man.

"Ever hear of DePaul?"

"In Chicago?"

"The very same. Point guard, 1987. Didn't make All American or anything, but I played some."

"What's that got to do with me?"

"For you to make the team, you need to convince Thompson he'd be a fool to turn his back on you again. I think I can get you there."

"Yeah, right."

"We're not talking miracles kid, we're talking effort. You've already laid the groundwork. If you let me, I can build you into a better player."

Against the outline of the foothills, the boy and the priest climb out of the riverbed. The Indian watches the taller man walk vigorously towards the mission.

"Meet me at the high school next Monday night for open gym and we'll get started" Father Baraga says matter-of-factly without turning around.

Augustus shudders from the chilly night air. The teenager watches the cleric open the weatherworn door to the church and disappear. Left behind in the swirling purity of a high desert snow, the youth considers the power of unspoken prayer.

CUYUNA ANGEL

There were dykes on the girl's hockey team. Renee DeAngelis wasn't one of them. Even though she was only seventeen, she knew that her inclinations were orientated towards boys. The particulars of her leanings didn't detract from her ability to play the game.

She started skating on ponds around Crosby, a little town near Brainerd, Minnesota, located in the heart of the old Cuyuna Iron Range, when she was still in diapers. Her father, Steven, didn't push her. He simply took her with whenever Steve and Renee's older brother, Tony, headed for the rink. Rink is a misnomer. They skated, by and large, on ovals cleared on the surface of Rabbit Lake; a small pothole nestled in between the town of Crosby and the Mississippi River. Their house sat on a knoll thick with oaks and scrub maples overlooking the south shore of the lake. The DeAngelis family skating rink materialized every winter as a shimmering jewel, a rare gem, located just off the shoreline in front of their house.

Growing up, Renee and her best friend Mary Zupec played on boy's teams. The two girls, their long hair pressed tight under their hockey helmets during games, reveled in concealing their gender from their opponents. After a contest, win or lose, the girls would remove their headgear, shake their locks free, and walk up to the opposition as if there was nothing unusual about two girls playing ice hockey.

Through their last year of Pee Wees, when the girls became thirteen-year-old young ladies, they played with and against boys. That all changed when girl's high school hockey came to town.

Renee and Mary were the only real players on the girl's team from eighth grade, when they began their high school careers, until their junior year. Their teammates were an odd assortment of former figure skaters, female broomball fanatics, and unathletic young women who went out for the team because of sheer boredom. By the time Renee and Mary were in eleventh grade, a half-dozen decent players had emerged to form a strong Single A team, a team that many observers felt had a chance to play in the State Tournament in St. Paul.

But their junior year ended quickly when Proctor-Hermantown-Marshall, a unified squad from the same area of the state, ran over them in the section finals by a score of 7 to 2. Renee scored the two goals. Mary Zupec had an assist and two penalties. Zupec's infractions were assessed for checking in a no-check game, a residual habit from Mary's years of playing hockey with boys.

Entering their senior year, the team didn't lose any players of note. In fact, a set of twins, the McClellan sisters, girls who'd grown up in St. Paul and played for Hill-Murray, a private school, moved in. Talk around Crosby, at the coffee shops and in the barber's chairs, was that this was the year; this was the team to make a run at a state championship.

Coach Ethan Dugas worked the girls hard. His expectations for them were high. The pressure on him to perform in his fifth year as head coach was mounting. It was clear to even casual fans that Dugas' job was on the line. If the team didn't make state, he was finished as its coach.

Just before Christmas break, Mary Zupec began to miss practice. Her mom, Helen, and her mom's partner, Joyce Simmons, had been together, running the Rabbit Lake Resort, for a decade or more, ever since Mary's old man took off for the Cities with a waitress from the Sandhill Tap in Cuyuna. The scandal of a forty-two-year-old father and husband running off with a twenty-year-old high school drop out couldn't hold a candle to what happened in the wake of Mitch Zupec's desertion.

There'd been rumors flying around the played-out mining communities of the Cuyuna Range long before Joyce moved in with Helen. Whispers at Mass, knowing looks from Crosby's socially elevated patriarchs and matriarchs. Cruel gossip preceded the women finalizing their living arrangement.

Mary knew early on that her mother was attracted to women. That her father and her mom had stayed together for twenty years and had a kid was, to Mary's thinking, nothing short of miraculous. There was no love; no affection shown between her parents beyond casual greetings and perfunctory pecks on the cheek. There was no fire, no desire raging for each other. As young as Mary was when her dad took off, she realized his departure was inevitable.

Most of the town folk let the scandal of the lesbian relationship die a natural death. People's initial shock at learning of the union between the women gave way to acceptance by the vast majority of Crosby's residents. Mass, however, was impossible. Though life-long Catholics, the women chose to attend a little Methodist church located outside of town. The few murmurs of outrage that surfaced when the couple first appeared for Sunday services at the Methodist church died away once members of the congregation got to know and appreciate the women.

The lump on Helen's left breast changed things, changed the routine of running the resort, changed the household. If there'd been only a mastectomy to deal with, Joyce and Mary, the two charged with picking up the slack for Helen, could have handled the extra work. An ultrasound of Helen's pelvis revealed that the cancer had metastasized into her uterus. She was dying. There would be no respite from the constant work around the resort.

"You can't keep missing practice and expect to be part of this team," Coach Dugas said one day, noting that Mary Zupec had missed two 6:00am starts.

"I'm sorry. My mom isn't feeling well."

In the center of the ice, under the artificial lights of the Crosby Community Center Arena, Dugas stood over his diminutive defenseman, one of only four girls remaining from his first team. His hands, protected by distressed hockey gloves that he'd worn as a college player, grasped a wooden stick. The blade of the appliance, heavily cushioned with black electrician's tape, rested on the ice. Dugas' legs were spread apart. The coach's weight leaned heavily on the stick as he listened to the girl. All the other players were in the locker room.

"I've heard about your mother."

There was a hint of unkind judgment lurking in the man's words. The girl noticed the prejudice but chose to ignore it. Her attention was riveted on the admonition that she knew was coming.

"Do you want to play on this team or not?"

A look of anxiety crossed Mary's eyes as the veiled threat registered in her mind.

"Yes," she replied, her voice nearly inaudible.

"Then you better get yourself to practice."

There was a period of prolonged silence. The coach studied the face of his player.

"That'll be all."

"But..."

"I said, that'll be all."

The coach's eyes glared from beneath the brim of his "Fighting Sioux" baseball cap.

"Get off the ice and get dressed."

Mary pulled her stick into her chest, raised the blade off the ice and skated towards the locker room.

"What happened?"

Renee DeAngelis watched as Zupec threw her graphite stick across the room before sitting down hard on the wooden bench in front of the varsity lockers. A single tear descended from Zupec's left eye. Mary wiped the moisture away with the sweat stained sleeve of her practice jersey. She did not answer. The rest of the team had showered and left the building.

"What did coach say?"

DeAngelis coated her words with kindness. The hockey player reduced the insistence of her tone.

"He said I can't miss any more practices."

"Your mom's sick. Doesn't the asshole know that?"

"He knows it. I didn't tell him but Principal Marcus did."

"Can't he cut you some slack?"

Renee removed her shin guards and threw them into the back of her locker. Plastic slammed against metal with violence.

"What are you gonna do?"

There was pause.

"Try to make it to the six am's," Mary replied.

Renee stared at her companion's face in disbelief. She'd been over to the Zupec house. She knew that Helen was fading fast, that Mary's mom had maybe another three weeks of life left in her at best. The hockey player's anger soared. Her disdain for Dugas, the coach that she'd grown up with, began to raise a bitter taste in her mouth.

"Are you nuts? You're hardly able to get a couple hours sleep a night. Why is Dugas doing this?"

Mary raised her eyes and looked blankly at her friend.

"Because my mom's gay."

"He said that?"

"Not in so many words. But it gets around. I've heard that he's never been all that fond of having the daughter of a lesbian on his team. Thinks I might try to put the moves on my teammates or somethin'."

DeAngelis placed her hand on Mary's moisture soaked T-Shirt. Sweat coated her friend's hair. There was an unpleasant odor of confined perspiration about them both.

"That's bullshit. I've known you since you were a little kid. I know you're not that way."

"But that doesn't stop the talk."

"You and I both know there are at least three girls on this team who bat from the other side of the plate. And you're not one of them. Besides, what the hell does that have to do with anything?"

"All I know is that I better make practice or my ass is grass."

There was a note of hopelessness to the girl's voice as she shed the last of her clothes and headed towards the shower.

Things didn't get any better. Helen needed more and more morphine. Tumors, tracked and cataloged by CT scan, showed up on her spine, making rest impossible without massive doses of narcotics. Joyce became ineffective. There had been an over abundance of new snow in January making the snowmobiling the best it had been in three years. Hundreds of tourists from the Twin Cities converged on the area in search of new trails to ride. They all needed food and lodging. Joyce simply wasn't up to meeting the visitor's demands.

Instead, she began a vigil. She took to her rocking chair, sitting next to Helen, watching the deep brown eyes of her lover lose vitality and color. Mary had to remind Joyce to shower, to undertake minimum personal hygiene rituals. All of the daughter's time became occupied with her mother's dying and with taking care of her mother's lover. More practices were missed.

Dugas remained silent. The girls continued to play well, beating Duluth Denfeld, a large school with a well-established program, in a weekend tournament. Mary had two assists. Renee had a hat trick. Elsa, one of the twins, picked up the other goal. Heading into the playoffs, Crosby was a respectable 15-5 and seeded number one in the section.

Renee DeAngelis had matured into a dominant player. Her senior year, she amassed 37 goals and 23 assists, the third highest point total in the state. More than her point production, Renee's speed and moves defined her as a premier competitor. She was nominated for the State's "Ms. Hockey" award and became one of five finalists for the honor. Colleges began to call.

Because of her small size, five-three and one hundred and ten pounds, Division One schools were hesitant to offer her a full ride. Dugas said they were waiting to see how well she did in the playoffs before getting serious. Most of the elite college programs had one or two open scholarships, slots that hadn't been snapped up early in the recruiting year, for players who achieved late-season success. The Coach told her to shoot for one of those.

Practices over the weekend had been a bear. DeAngelis' legs burned when she walked into the arena at 5:00am on Monday morning. She was the first one there besides the coach. She waved at Dugas as he sat doing paperwork in his office, his door slightly ajar so he could keep an eye on things. The coach ignored her.

Renee's eyes were drawn to the team bulletin board. There was a large yellow piece of paper with the heading "Tournament Roster" typed in bold black letters across the notice. Renee approached the board and began to read the names. Mary Zupec wasn't listed.

"Hey Coach, there's a mistake on the roster."

DeAngelis stood in red sweat pants and a blue "Duke University" sweatshirt, her hair pulled back and tied up off her neck, just outside the coach's office. Her eyes studied Dugas' face. She curled and uncurled her stocking covered feet in anxious anticipation of his attention.

"How so?"

"Mary's not on the list."

"That surprises you?"

181

Dugas didn't engage the player with his eyes as he continued to study the papers on the metal desk in front of him.

"She's one of the best players on the team. She's leading the defense in plus-minus."

"And she can't get her ass here for practice. I warned her, DeAngelis. I gave her time to get her act together. She hasn't done squat since I talked to her. I'm going with Robin as the fourth D."

The coach's reference to sometime starter Robin Winters as Mary's replacement drew Renee's ire.

"What? Winters' is only a freshman. She doesn't have the game Zupec has. She might in a couple of years. But not now."

"I've made my decision. Get yourself dressed. Practice starts in half an hour."

Other girls filtered into the locker room. In groups of twos and threes, they stopped in front of the roster sheet to assure themselves they were suiting up for the playoffs.

DeAngelis walked over to the bench in front of her locker. Mary was already there and crying.

"That son of a bitch," Renee said, loosely placing her hand on her friend's right forearm. "That asshole has no right to do this. If I were you, I'd go to Principal Marcus and have Dugas' ass thrown right out of this school."

Mary's sobs echoed across the metal doors of the lockers. Renee's eyes met those of her teammate. Without uttering a word, Mary rose and began walking towards the door. Before Renee could stop her, the hockey player was gone.

Practice was a disaster. The older members of the team didn't accept Winters as a replacement for their comrade. Dugas yelled, cajoled, and screamed at the girls as he tried to run the team through drills. After an hour of frustration, the coach took the pucks away and skated the team without respite. In school that morning, most of the players were too tired to stay awake in class.

Thursday evening. Game time: 7:00pm at the Crosby rink. Crosby-Ironton-Aitkin versus Brainerd. The first playoff game. CIA had bested Brainerd by significant margins twice during the year. There was little doubt amongst the Crosby faithful as to the game's outcome.

Around the dinner table at the DeAngelis house, there was an absence of gaiety. Steve and Ardith, Renee's parents, sat at opposite ends of the harvest table. Tony and Renee were positioned in chairs across from each other. The boy stabbed at pot roast, green beans, and mashed potatoes, piled high on his plate, with a fork. His mouth devoured food in gulps. Renee picked at her meal. She was obviously distracted.

"What's wrong, angel?" her father asked. His eyes looked over his eyeglasses as he spoke. A copy of the Minneapolis Tribune rested on the tabletop next to his forearm. Steven's eyes had been riveted on the sports page. Now he concentrated his attention on his daughter.

"You need to eat. The game's not for another two hours. You'll have plenty of time to digest. Just don't fill yourself up," Ardith counseled.

Renee's long hair had been recently cut. She'd gone to a more severe style. The change made her look five years older than seventeen. She wore a bright red hand-knit sweater, blue jeans, and white anklets but no shoes. The sweater was too big for her frame. It rode on her narrow shoulders like a tent. She was slight of waist, ample through the hips, with a modest bust, slightly rounded jaw, light hazel eyes, and a dimpled smile when she chose to share it.

"She's pissed off at the coach," her brother related.

Tony managed to spit out the words without disgorging the majority of his dinner.

"That right?"

Her dad's eyes narrowed, concentrating their powerful blue centers on his daughter as he inquired.

"What's up?"

"She's upset that Mary isn't playing," Ardith interjected.

"To hell you say. When did that happen?"

"Steven, watch your language. She's known about it all week. I didn't tell you because I thought you might over react."

"Ya, dad. We thought you might go over and cold cock Coach Dugas," Tony chuckled.

Color pulsed across Steven DeAngelis' face.

"What right does he have to do that? The poor girl is losing her mother and he benches her? For what?"

"For missing too many practices," his wife whispered.

"What in the world are you saying, Ardith? That he's booted her off the team because her mom is sick and needs help?"

"That's the way Renee tells it."

"Renee? Is that right?"

The girl's eyes focused forward, revealing a defiant, piercing attitude. Her father recognized the stare. It was the same look Renee got whenever Tony schooled her on the ice rink when they were younger.

"That's what Dugas told me."

"Isn't Joyce gonna do something about it? Talk to Ed Marcus? Call the School Board?"

"Honey, Joyce isn't herself. With Helen barely hanging on, the last thing that Joyce is capable of is going to bat for Mary," Ardith observed.

"We gotta do something. I can't just sit here and let my daughter's best friend, and one heckofa good kid, get the shaft."

Renee DeAngelis stood up and placed her paper napkin on the pine surface of the table. She spoke in a quiet, mature tone:

"I am doing something about it. I'm not dressing tonight."

Her father frowned.

"You've got to be kidding. There are better ways of getting your point across than giving up a college scholarship. Let's think this through," Steven implored, the edge in his voice disappearing as he spoke.

"My mind's made up. I won't put one skate on the ice for that asshole coach. There's more to life than playing hockey."

"Think what you're saying, Renee. You've worked so hard; your father has worked so hard to get you here. Dad's right, maybe there's something else we can do to get Mary reinstated," Ardith implored.

"It's too late. Dugas turned in the tournament roster on Monday after he posted it. Mary couldn't play even if every player on the team sat down on the ice and demanded it. This is the only thing I can do for her."

"But...."

The teenager did not linger to hear her father's admonition. She left the kitchen. Her gait increased. Passing a coat rack, Renee removed her letter jacket from a peg, pulled the sleeves over her arms and walked out the backdoor of the log house.

Mary Zupec sat on the edge of a bed cloaked in feeble light in her mother's bedroom reading a passage from the novel *The Book of Ruth* aloud. Helen's eyes were shut. She was neither asleep nor dead; she was concentrating against the pain, battling a hurt so intense that morphine no longer did the job, to listen to the story. Joyce sat in her chair, knitting a stocking cap.

"Can I come in?"

Mary stopped reading from Jane Hamilton's novel when she recognized the voice of her best friend. A clock sitting on a dresser claimed it was 6:15pm. The game would be starting in forty-five minutes. Warm-ups had already begun. Mary Zupec looked up, her feet coiled beneath her, her luxurious black hair loose and flowing

185

down the back of her sweater. Her voice betrayed a lack of understanding:

"You're supposed to be at the arena."

"I'm not playing tonight."

"What the hell are you talking about?" Mary responded in a loud voice, a voice inappropriate for a hospice room.

"Shhhhh. Keep it down. Renee, why aren't you at the game?" Joyce asked.

"I won't play for Coach Dugas."

"Because of what he did to me?" Mary replied. "That's stupid. I wasn't going anywhere in hockey after high school anyway. It isn't that big of a deal."

"You're a senior, the best defenseman on the team, and my best friend. It's a big deal to me."

Sobs erupted. Mary rose from the bed, walked the short distance to where Renee stood in the doorway, and slipped her arms around her friend's body. The visitor reciprocated. Both girls wept significantly.

"I can't believe you did this for me."

"I didn't do so much. I should have been here, we all should have been here as a team, taking turns with your mom. Then you wouldn't have been cut. I'm sorry."

Mary's face turned to look at her mother. Helen's eyes opened. Tears formed and pooled in the crevices of her cheeks.

"That girl is one hell of a friend," the dying woman murmured. "You better not forget this."

"I won't, mom. I won't," Mary replied.

Crosby beat Brainerd 2-1. The twins scored the goals on breakaways. In the next game, Park Rapids pounded CIA 5-0. The season was over. Dugas was removed from his coaching position immediately after the loss. His non-tenured physical education position was eliminated at the end of the school year.

Helen Zupec died the day after Renee DeAngelis made her stand. Mary was in the kitchen, making lunch, as her friend finished reading the Hamilton novel to the stricken woman. When Renee stood up from the rocking chair to stretch her hamstrings, her attention was diverted to a large flock of red winged blackbirds gathering over Rabbit Lake. Thoughts of spring and her Senior Prom date with David Andrews, the captain of the boy's hockey team, momentarily distracted her.

As the girl turned her attention back to the patient, Helen's Zupec's eyes fluttered, then closed. No exhalations stirred the linens covering the body, though a slight smile remained across the dead woman's lips, a smile that Renee DeAngelis would never forget.

A QUIET MAN

George Armstrong Rintala had been a jailer at the Carlton County jail for as long as most folks in the County could remember. He fell into the job after he returned home to Minnesota from the Korean War. He really wanted to be a cop on the beat but the pay at the lock-up came easier. His MP training, a strong Finnish physique, and a quick wit were all he needed to secure the job. He started as an assistant to the head jailer. Within five years, he was placed in charge of the facility after his mentor developed a drinking problem and didn't show up for work. At age seventy-three, George was finally slowing down, contemplating retirement.

He'd seen all kinds come through the iron doors of the old jail, and more recently, through the solid steel panels of the new Law Enforcement Center. There were young women, prostitutes from the Twin Cities that somehow got turned around and convinced they could make more money walking the streets of Cloquet, Minnesota than they could trolling the mangy watering holes of Minneapolis and St. Paul. Trouble was, and George saw it as soon as the matron checked the whores into the jail: the women's garish hair styles, piercings, tattoos, and outfits that seemed common-place in a metropolis stood out in Carlton County like red paint on a white fence.

Then there were the serious thugs; murderers, rapists, and high-level drug dealers who were always conspicuous in such a small jurisdiction. These customers formed a steady stream of business and kept Jailer Rintala's staff fully engaged.

During weekends, the place filled up quickly as drunk drivers, folks of all ages, body types, races, and economic status, crowded into the cells. Most came and went discretely, never to return for any other violation.

Through the years, the jail also secured its share of mentally incompetent, chemically dependent, and mentally ill folks that, due to the closure of long-term residential facilities throughout the state, wandered about on public streets until they did something to draw law enforcement attention to themselves.

Drops of rain slammed into the hard metal of his squad car as Carlton County Deputy Douglas Evans, one of two Native American officers on the force, drove north on Interstate 35 towards the Black Bear Casino. There was slight traffic on the road. The weather was fierce; the downpour, unrelenting.

"What the hell is he doing?" the deputy asked himself. Evans studied a man standing in the grassy median of the freeway. "He's gotta be half nuts."

Evans turned on the red overhead lights of his squad and slowed the car. As he pulled onto the left edge of the roadway, the deputy opened the driver's side window:

"Hey buddy," he shouted over the din of the water striking his car, "what do you think you're doing?"

The man didn't respond.

"Dispatch, this is 23. I'm stopped northbound on I-35 just south of the viaduct by the Carlton Exit. There's some idiot standing in the damn rain in the middle of the median. I'm gonna try to coax him into the squad."

"Roger that, 23. 57 is en route and will be there to assist."

"Buddy, why don't you come in out of the rain so we can talk?" the officer shouted in a loud but non-threatening voice. The man continued to ignore the cop's pleas. The stranger was dressed in a pair of faded blue jeans and a white linen shirt. His feet were bare and muddy. His shirt was soaked through, making the skin of his chest, his nipples and his torso, visible through the cloth. His hair, thick and reddish brown, hung heavily across the collar of his shirt, soaked through as it was by precipitation. With deliberation, the man raised his arms to the sky, turning his palms upward to the storm as his wrists extended above his shoulders.

"Shit," Evans muttered. "I'm gonna have to drag the crazy somebitch in out of the rain."

The deputy exited the squad car. Immediately, his uniform was soaked through. Red light accented the immediate atmosphere as the emergency beacons of the police unit flashed behind him. Evans approached the man. The officer's right hand rested easily on the butt of his holstered pistol.

"What seems to be the problem, sir?"

There was no response.

"I'm asking you if something's wrong."

There was no reaction from the man. Another car arrived. Joyce Tortelli, a rookie with the department, exited her squad and approached.

"What's up, Evans?"

Rain dripped off the Indian's broad head. His bald spot was slick and shiny from the moisture.

"I can't get a word outahim," Evans responded. "He hasn't moved a muscle since I walked over here."

The quiet man stood, his eyes closed and mystical, his hands uplifted towards heaven, as water cascaded down his body in torrents.

"Hey fella," Tortelli yelled, her voice bright and crisp, "What's your name?"

Silence.

"If you don't tell us your name, we're gonna have to haul you in for obstructing. We don't want to have to do that," the female officer advised.

Nothing.

"Let's get him the hell out of here before he takes off out into traffic and gets himself killed," Deputy Evans recommended.

The woman nodded. Advancing slowly towards the man, Tortelli maintained her gaze on his facial features. She tried to gauge what his reaction would be when she got close enough to put her hands on him. He was somewhere around thirty, clean shaven, and pleasant looking. The female deputy didn't have a clue as to the color of his eyes because he hadn't opened his eyelids.

"Watch him, Evans. I think he's a little touched. Be ready to jump in if I need ya."

She placed a hand on the soaked fabric of the man's shirtsleeve. The man didn't react. With steady pressure, pressure that was met with no resistance, she brought each arm down and behind the subject's back. His eyes remained closed, his head, uplifted, his facial expression void of recognition, as she handcuffed him.

"This here's one weird dude."

Her partner's comment floated past Tortelli's ears on the back of the storm.

"You got that right."

George Rintala helped inventory the man's clothing and possessions when the stranger was processed. The jailer had a difficult time undoing the suspect's barndoor. Arthritis had long-since curled the thumb and forefingers of Rintala's hands creating an unnatural scissoring of digits.

"Damn it," the old man muttered. "Aspirin ain't worth a shit," he complained as he fumbled with the zipper.

The prisoner carried no wallet, no money, nothing to aid the jailers in determining who he was. Once showered, a task the stranger didn't resist or assist, the man simply sat on the corner of his bunk in his cell. His eyes had opened during the shower. But as hot water washed his nakedness, he never blinked. The blue of his eyes stared blankly at those around him, seemingly absent any sign of comprehension.

Miles Dougherty, the Assistant County Attorney charged with prosecuting the case, didn't object when Judge McClellan ordered "The Man with Blue Eyes", as the defendant became known, evaluated at the state mental health facility in Brainerd.

"Seems appropriate," was all Miles said during the hearing.

Eustace Putika, "Blue Eyes'" public defender, made the request for the evaluation when her client wouldn't talk to her, wouldn't even acknowledge her presence in the jail conference room where they met to discuss the obstructing charge.

"He hasn't said a word or made a gesture that shows he's aware of the proceedings or even that he understands what planet he's on," she observed in support of her demand.

"Tough to represent a client who's in a psychological coma, counselor. We'll see what they come up with in Brainerd," the judge had remarked.

"They're sending you off to Brainerd for an evaluation," George Rintala said softly as he pulled the sleeves of a freshly laundered and pressed shirt over "Blue Eyes'" hands and wrists. "Maybe someone there can make a connection with you. I've seen all sorts of fellas in here during my time. But I've never met anyone quite like you."

The man remained seated on the bench, allowing the garment to be pulled over his arms, again, not assisting and not resisting the jailer's efforts in any way.

"I've been meaning to ask you, not that you're gonna answer. Where'd you get these nasty scars?"

Old George touched the palms of the man's hands as he asked the question. At the junction of each hand and wrist were large, circular areas of smooth scar tissue. The jailer wanted to ask about the nasty gash across the man's stomach he'd discovered when "Blue Eyes" first disrobed, before his first shower in the facility, as well. Given the lack of response from his charge, Rintala gave up further inquiry.

"He hasn't said a single word in the entire week he's been with us, George."

Eddie Thompson, the Assistant Jailer, stepped into the cell as he spoke:

192

"I've got his transport order right here. Two weeks in Brainerd. Maybe they can come up with something. Seems sad to see a person this way. He's here, I mean, his eyes react, it appears he knows what's going on around him, but there's no words, no glimmer of deeper understanding."

Rintala stared hard into the face of the prisoner.

"Strangest bird I've ever met," the jailer whispered. "Kinda spooky, but in a non-threatening fashion, if you know what I mean."

"I get that same vibe off him, like he's simply waiting for something to happen to him, like he has no control over his own life," Thompson agreed.

Judge McClellan held the commitment hearing at the local hospital. Brainerd had returned the accused man after a full work up. An identification had been made. "Blue Eyes" was really Francis Delmor, a drifter from Missouri who'd been in and out of mental health facilities across the Midwest, most often for "excessive religiosity" and "delusions" related to the anticipated return of the Messiah.

"What's the position of the county? It's clear he's not fit to go to trial on the criminal charge. And I'm not so sure his refusal to cooperate with deputies even comes close to obstruction. What do you say, Mr. Dougherty?" the judge asked.

The hearing was held in the conference room of the Carlton County Medical Center just outside the city limits. A social worker; Ms. Putika representing the accused; Miles Dougherty appearing for the State as the prosecutor; Dr. Powers, the staff psychiatrist; a mental health floor security guard; the court reporter; the judge; and of course, Francis Delmor, occupied chairs located around a large conference table.

"I agree that the criminal case is thin and likely won't amount to much but I'm concerned about Mr. Delmor being released into the community. He's been

193

speaking a little since he came back from Brainerd and quite frankly, I think he needs a short term commitment here at the hospital to deal with his delusions."

"Judge, I've read Dr. Powers' follow-up assessment," Ms. Putika interjected. "While he notes that Mr. Delmore remains somewhat delusional, he also notes that he's non-violent, surely not a danger to society. He's well nourished and has been taking care of his daily living needs without assistance. The fact that he's religious, even hyper-religious, is no reason to keep him locked up in a psyche ward."

"Doctor, is that your assessment?"

The judge, a man, like Jailer Rintala, on the verge of retirement, looked over his trifocals as he queried the psychiatrist. The judge's bald head moist with sweat. The few remaining strands of white along the back of his neck were neatly secured in place with an overabundance of hair tonic.

"That's fairly close. I'd like to keep him in the hospital for further observation but I can't say that he's a danger to himself or anyone else," the psychiatrist replied.

"Then the law says he must be released. Mr. Delmor, I find that there is an insufficient factual basis to commit you and, as soon as you can be processed by the jail, you're free to go about your business."

Delmor looked at the aging judge with patient eyes. His mouth opened briefly, as if he wanted to utter a word of thanks. Nothing came out. The accused simply sighed and looked out a near-by window.

"Here, you're gonna need this," Rintala whispered, handing the prisoner two twenty dollar bills as they headed towards the exit to the Carlton County Law Enforcement Center. "Get something to eat and a good jacket before you head back out on the road. It's summer, but the nights around here can be mighty cold."

Delmore stood next to the old man, his hands to his side, expressionless and quiet. The jailer's deformed right hand pushed the crumpled currency into the soft palm of his charge. When the old man sought to retreat, the vagrant's grip tightened. George Rintala's face expressed surprise at the strength of the smaller man's grasp:

"Hey, that's some handshake you got there, pal."

Francis Delmore did not release his grip. The jailer felt a surge of warmth engage his palm. Unnatural heat pulsed through Rintala's hand. It was as if the appendage was on fire, and yet, somehow vastly different. The stranger's face relaxed. The old man looked into the bottomless blue of Delmor's eyes and thought he saw something there, thought he recognized the man as someone he knew long ago, when the jailer was a child. The image vanished. The odd sensation in Rintala's hand abated.

"Thanks," the wanderer said, shoving the bills into his shirt pocket as he walked out the door.

That same day, George Rintala felt the arthritic ache in his joints begin to subside. Within a week, the jailer was swinging a golf club and carving intricate wooden mallard decoys like a young man.

STERLING, COLORADO

She was a plain looking girl with an extraordinary mind living an ordinary life.

Lucinda Clark sat on a hay bale, the fibers dry and prickly against the bare skin of her ankles. Her hazel eyes scanned the valley of the South Platte River flowing meagerly through the drought-impacted landscape. The knoll she occupied was littered with several hundred bales of hay cut for the upcoming winter. The squares were strewn randomly across the stubble of a mown alfalfa field no more than two hundred feet above the river's course. The promontory climbed from the banks of the stream to Lucy's vantage point in gradual fashion.

She was dressed in denim jeans. Lucinda favored Lee's, straight-legged and baggy around the legs despite her solid shape. She wore a long sleeved "Colorado Avalanche" sweatshirt, and beat-up discount store tennis shoes. Seventeen-years-old and a senior at Sterling High School, Lucinda Clark was amply chested, more so than she liked, boasting shiny brown hair with auburn highlights that, when they caught the sunshine, sparkled like rare gems under a jeweler's lamp. The color of her eyes matched the hue of the prairie sky standing thin over the grasslands surrounding her family's ranch.

It had been a tough day at school. No one understood her. She wished that her mother was still around but Gayle Clark was living somewhere down south, near Santa Fe or thereabouts, having met a man, a poet that she claimed to be in love with. They'd bumped into each other, leading, apparently, to a lot more serious-type bumping into each other, when Dale Eckhardson gave a reading at the Tattered Cover Bookstore in Cherry Creek last February. Gayle began to sneak around, making more and more obvious excuses to escape the smallness of Sterling for the bustle of

Denver at odd times, seemingly during the moments when Lucinda needed her mother the most.

The girl's eyes were fixed steady as she watched a herd of Black Angus mosey from dry patch of grass to dry patch of grass. Her eyes seemed locked on the cattle but her mind was on other things.

Harold Clark, the girl's father, tried hard with Melinda, Lucy's ten-year-old sister, and Lucy, tried to fill in the emptiness and the void left by their departed mother. He wasn't much good at the empathy and soul-unburdening part of that equation, though he took a concerted stab at it when asked. Mostly, Lucy found herself turning inward or to God when she had questions. She tried to help Melinda out as much as she could, imparting whatever wisdom her seventeen years of life could impart.

The thing at school troubled her. For the first time it pitted her humanity against the Divine in clear and contentious ways.

"Ms. Clark, what do you think of President Bush's response to the events of September 11?" Mrs. Blanchard, her 12th grade civics teacher, had asked during second hour.

The class was deep in the midst of hashing out what should constitute an appropriate military response to the terrible acts of Bin Ladin and his cohorts when the question came her way. The conversation up to that point had been directed by the boys in her class:

"We oughta nuke those stinking towel heads back to the Stone Age," Benny Morrison had postulated.

"Benny, are you suggesting we use atomic weapons on Afghanistan, against innocent women and children?" Mrs. Blanchard had interjected.

"Why stop there? I'd blast every last freakin Muslim country on the planet. Let 'em know who's boss."

"That's bogus," Emitt Carlson chimed in. "Some of the Muslim countries are our allies, like Saudi Arabia."

Benny grinned:

"Ya, but if we blew them to little pieces, we wouldn't have to beg them for oil. Plus, that's where Bin Ladin and most of the suicide guys came from. I say nuke 'em."

The discourse centered upon military tactics; upon the necessity of sending in American ground troops; of what the public's reaction would likely be to scenes of dead American soldiers, men and women, coming home in body bags. Through it all, Lucinda Clark, the brightest kid in the senior class and usually one of the first to join a debate, maintained her own counsel.

When the question was finally turned in Lucy's direction, she understood why the teacher wanted the girl involved. The Clark's were Friends. Quakers. Pacifism was an integral part of her family's faith. There was history here, in little Sterling: an invisible line ran between the three Quaker families located in and around the town and their neighbors. Mrs. Blanchard clearly knew that history and was drawing upon it to spur a lively discussion.

Trouble was, Lucinda, normally eager to swagger into a verbal fray, wanted to shrivel up and disappear rather than discuss the finer points of America's response to September 11th. The reasons weren't complex. The reasons were simple. Somehow, what had taken place in the peaceful autumnal atmosphere over New York City on that fateful day was so vastly different, so incomprehensibly evil, when considered by a seventeen-year-old young woman from a Colorado ranching community, that the old guideposts and measures of her religion no longer seemed useful.

"Lucy?" the teacher had repeated, staring hard at the young woman's face, a clear pronunciation of understanding in her gaze.

The girl's eyes moistened slightly as she watched Beau Gunderson, the next-door neighbor's seventeen-year-old son, lope across the dusty grassland on a spirited black and white paint towards the cattle. The Angus stood complacently, their heads turning in unison towards the on-rushing cowboy, the slope of their strong, thick backs appearing as dark lumps against the yellow ground.

She studied the far reaches of the valley, where newly turned soil appeared black. The dirt would eventually dry beneath the unfamiliar November sun and turn the color of coal ash; becoming nearly identical in color to the powder that settled over the horror-stricken faces of the people Lucinda watched escape the collapse of the Twin Towers on network television news.

"Yes, ma'am," she had answered.

"I know you must have something to say about what's happening in Central Asia."

"Not really."

The teacher's eyes flared though her temper didn't rise.

"Surely you have something to add regarding what will likely turn out to be the most memorable event of your generation," Mrs. Blanchard coaxed.

"Come on, Luce," Barton Morales, one of a handful of Hispanics in her grade, chided. "You're always ready to give an opinion, even if it's bogus," he added, a wide grin showing white against tawny skin.

Others added their derisions.

Lucinda drew a deep breath and thought of a response:

"Let's say that Bin Ladin, and maybe even the Taliban, is responsible for what happened," she began.

"Maybe? Where you been hiding girl, in a cave?" Carla Morales, Barton's twin sister castigated. "They've got old Bin Ladin dead to rights. All that's left is the finale in his sorry little one-act play."

Lucy smiled. She liked Carla, liked her assuredness and her natural ability to cut to the chase.

"Fair enough. Suppose, instead of sending 50,000 Special Forces to Afghanistan to fight the Taliban, we send a couple of hundred thousand civilians: men, women, kids like us, over to Pakistan. Then we all march across the border, unarmed, seeking a parlay with the Taliban. Do you really believe that they are so inhumane, so brutal, that they'd attack us?"

Missy Forestall, a cheerleader and a short, finely proportioned blond with athletic thighs and deep brown eyes set in an exquisite face, laughed:

"Carla's right. You've completely lost it if you think those animals would be willing to listen. Especially to women. Don't you follow the news? Don't you understand how they beat, mistreat, and subjugate women?"

Lucinda's mouth turned. Mrs. Blanchard attempted to reassert control.

"Keep your critique positive, folks," she admonished. "I see you have your hand up, Edgar. Go ahead."

Edgar Brewster, a slow thinking, large-boned tackle on the varsity football team cleared his throat. His voice was soft, at odds with his stature:

"I dunno. Maybe Lucy's got something here."

Noisy objections erupted from the class. The instructor raised her hand.

"Lucy?"

Thin strips of white, fingers extending two-dimensionally from a bank of high clouds resting to the north, up near Cheyenne, reached across the high atmosphere. The rancher's daughter detected the beginnings of the foothills from her perch, gentle peaks immediately adjacent to Fort Collins, visible though seventy miles away as the crow flies. The spine of hills rose above the flatness of the western terminus of the prairie as a magnificent apparition.

"God, why did it happen?" she asked softly, a faint breeze beginning to stir. The answer, she knew, was in the hearts of men and not in the mind of God.

At the edge of the Gunderson pasture, Beau and his Border collie, Blue, drove cattle through an open gate towards a watering station. Several hundred yards away, a windmill spun violently despite the meager wind. A horse neighed from the ridge behind her.

"Obligation," she murmured, turning her head, her hair jostling as she moved. She whistled to her horse.

A blaze of white broke across the drab landscape. Dust churned from beneath the Arab's hooves as the animal raced towards the girl, its shoulders undulating as it ran: its gray mane and tail trailing its effort.

Lucinda had formulated a feeble response to her teacher's inquiry.

"It's a puzzlement, to me, being Quaker and all. My faith tells me that war is something that, only in the most dire of circumstances, should be engaged in by humankind," the girl whispered weakly.

Mrs. Blanchard stood next to the young woman.

"Well, isn't this such a time?" Barton Morales challenged. "I mean, the son of a...excuse me, Ms. Blanchard...bee killed civilians. What we're doing isn't really going to war. It's more like a police manhunt."

There were murmurs of approval from other classmates.

"That's one way to look at it," Lucinda Clark demurred. "But what about all the Afghan women and children who'll be killed or hurt? Dropping bombs indiscriminately looks an awful lot like war to me."

"There's no right or wrong to any of your positions," Mrs. Blanchard concluded. "But I do think that Mr. Morales has brought up an interesting approach. If the acts that were committed were against civilians, isn't Barton right? Isn't this really a case of a criminal act and not an act of nation against nation, an act of war? Lucy, does that make sense to you?"

The young rancher pushed her body free of gravity and regained her feet. Stroking the soft nuzzle of the Arabian, her mind wandered from the death and the destruction, focusing instead upon an image of her mother.

Gayle Clark's eyes had been filled with sorrow and remorse as she sat behind the wheel of her Mazda 4x4, the vehicle's off-road tires worn smooth and resting in the gravel of their driveway. Melinda clutched the woman's hand, refusing to relinquish her grip, unwilling to let her mother leave. Finally, Lucinda stepped up and pulled her little sister away, the child convulsing in grief as the pick-up truck disappeared.

A strong odor of horse disbursed the memory. Lucinda stood quietly beside Obligation, massaging the horse's velvety skin, inhaling the animal's distinct musk. The young woman's eyes steadied on the flatness of the land. Footsteps echoing off the wind-hardened surface of the ground interrupted her thoughts.

"Thought I might find you up here," her father said as he approached from behind the girl, his lanky form in marked contrast to his eldest daughter's squat stature. Harold Clark's rugged face looked down kindly at his oldest child. His eyes, shadowed as they were by the brim of his Stetson, the off-white felt of the headgear worn and smudged from the business of ranching, looked diligently at Lucinda.

She pointed towards the Gunderson boy as horse and rider galloped across the plateau.

"I was just watching Beau and his dog work."

"Looks like Obie was giving you some comfort as you eavesdropped," the man remarked, dispensing a wad of chew into the warm air through tobacco-stained teeth.

Harold kept his eyes on his daughter.

"I'm worried about your baby sister," the rancher admitted, his words soft.

Lucy patted the belly of her horse and sent the animal off to graze.

"How so?"

"She doesn't seem to be coming out of her spin since your mother took off."

There was no sugar coating it. Their mother, his wife had done simply that. Taken off, leaving them all to fend for themselves with only intermittent telephone calls as the singular connection between them. Gayle didn't write or use the Internet. There were no letters, no emails, no photographs depicting Gayle's new life in New Mexico as a reminder to the girls that their mother cared.

"I guess," was all the girl replied.

"You seem troubled," Lucy's father observed, a task-roughened hand coming to rest on the back of her right wrist. "What's eating you?"

Lucinda thought about dodging the issue. Instead, she met the question head on:

"Dad, why do we have to be Quakers?"

A look of mild injury crept into her father's eyes:

"Why would you ask such a question?"

She shuffled her tennis shoes over the soft topsoil.

"Today at school we were talking about President Bush's response to the Trade Center thing. Everyone but me pretty much thought going to war over what happened was well within our rights."

The man's hand loosened on her arm.

"I see. What did you say in response?"

"Some lame suggestion that we send a few hundred thousand pilgrims over to Afghanistan to show Bin Ladin and the Taliban that we're peaceful, reasonable, God-fearing folk."

Wind blew her father's curly black hair loose of his neck and ears.

"Doesn't sound lame to me. Sounds like something Christ would say himself. Remember your scripture:

'To him who strikes you on the one cheek, offer the other also. And from him who takes away your cloak, do not withhold your tunic either. Love your enemies, do good, hoping for nothing in return.'

Luke, Chapter 6, Verses 29-35."

The young woman frowned and kicked at the ground:

"And what if what happened on September 11th wasn't an act of war but an act of murder?"

The man smiled:

"You really do need to go to law school, young lady. I see your point. Your argument has an attraction. But aren't you simply replacing the word 'war' with the word 'murder'?"

She returned the grin. It was the longest they'd spoken since her mother had left. Her eyes studied the tanned outlines of her father's profile against the glimmering sunset. Red, yellow, and gold tendrils ignited the western horizon. Shadows began to spread across the lowlands.

"Didn't Jesus also say 'render therefore to Caesar those things that are Caesar's and to God the things that are God's?'" she asked.

"Luke 20, Verse 25. But how does that relate to remaining a pacifist and steering clear of militarism?" the rancher postulated.

Lucy adjusted herself on the hay bale. Her father stretched his right leg, placing a well-worn cowboy boot on the alfalfa.

"If the law, which is Caesar's, requires a penalty to be paid for a crime, an earthly sin, shouldn't we then obey Caesar's law unless it speaks against our faith?" the girl asked.

Harold stroked the haggard skin of his chin, his jaw thick and prominent, the only portion of his face that mirrored his daughter's. He patted his child on the top of her shoulder.

"Girl, you really do need to go to law school," the cowboy muttered through a devilish grin.

The rancher and the young woman watched the sun settle over the Rocky Mountains. Dusk descended. Twilight faded. Evening prospered and crept eastward until it enveloped the rancher and his eldest daughter in night.

ABOUT THE AUTHOR

Mark Munger is a life long resident of Northeastern Minnesota. He and his wife Rene' and their four sons live on the banks of the wild and scenic Cloquet River north of Duluth. When not writing fiction, Mark writes a regular column for *The Hermantown Star* newspaper and is a Minnesota District Court Judge.

The Author and his son Christian, at Indian Lake, ready to begin a fifty mile canoe trip down the Cloquet River.

OTHER WORKS BY THE AUTHOR

The Legacy (ISBN 0972005021)

Set against the backdrop of World War II Yugoslavia and present-day Northeastern Minnesota, this debut novel combines elements of military history, romance, thriller, and mystery. Rated 3 and 1/2 daggers out of 4 by *The Mystery Review Quarterly*.
Trade Paperback $19.95

River Stories (ISBN 0972005013)

A collection of essays describing life in Northern Minnesota with a strong emphasis on the out-of-doors, the rearing of children, and the environment. A mixture of humor and thought-provoking prose gleaned from the author's columns in *The Hermantown Star*.
Trade Paperback-$19.95

Pigs, A Trial Lawyer's Story (ISBN 097200503X)

Munger's second novel combines literary fiction with contemporary sensibilities. This tale of love, the law, and choices made will likely strike a chord with readers of all stripes. Set in the Smokey Hills of Western Minnesota, **Pigs** chronicles the story of Danny Aitkins, a young trial lawyer, as he battles corporate greed and his own inner demons.
Available Nationwide February 1, 2003
Trade Paperback-$19.95